MOVIN' ON

ISBN: 978-0-6489302-1-1

Movin' On

A Teenage Poet, a Small Town, a Big Dream

DENIS R. GRAY

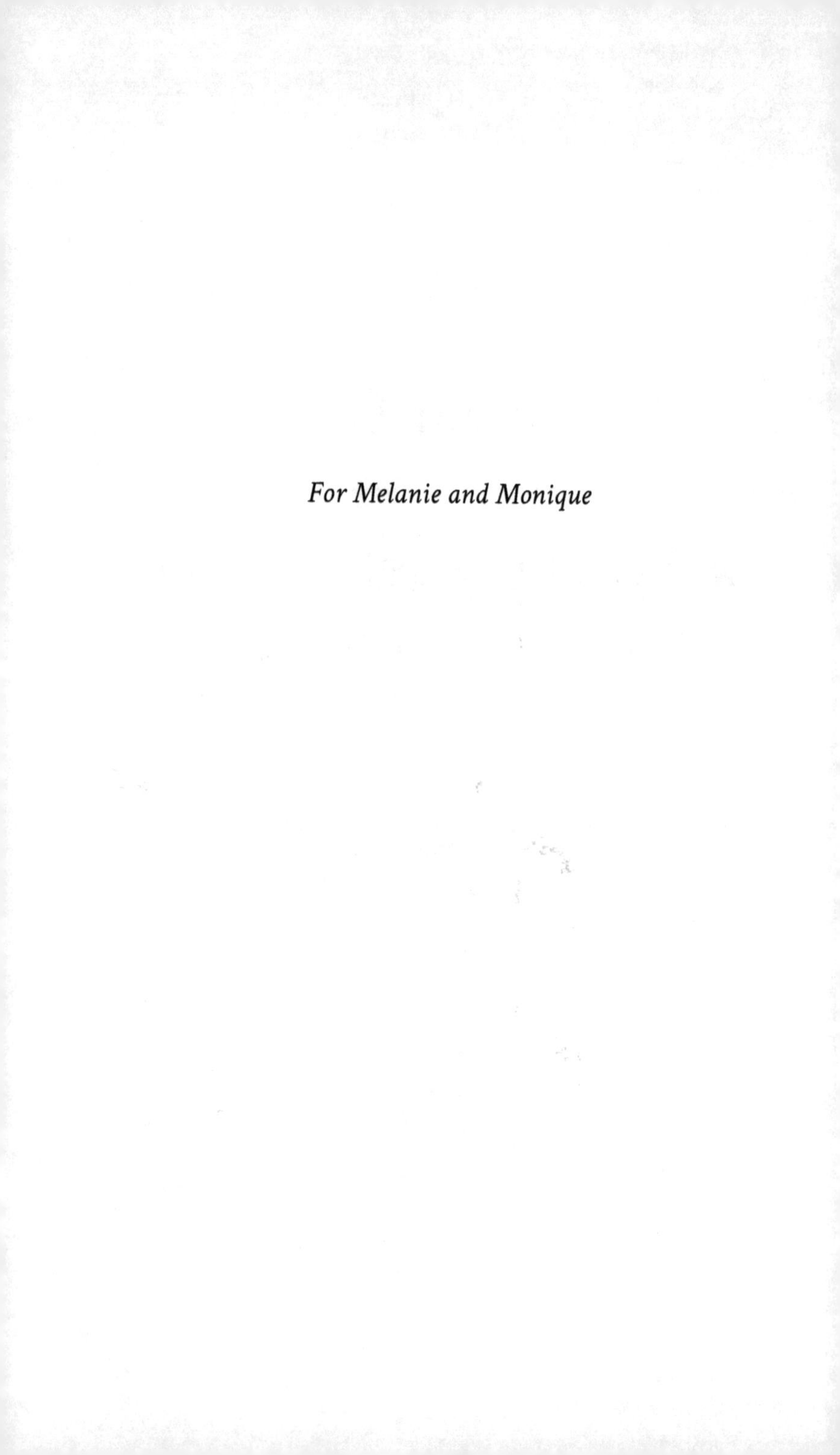

For Melanie and Monique

CONTENTS

| 1 |

Will you go to the dance with me ?

The Monday morning light broke through the curtains and slowly crawled up his face. His eyelids flickered three or four times before his hand slapped the clock radio, which was belting out its morning call.

'Disco at *this* time of the morning.' he murmured and flopped out of bed. Standing in front of a dis-coloured mirror he scratched his head, glanced at the clock, and shrieked loudly, 'A quarter past nine, it can't be!' In a matter of minutes, he flung on his clothes from last Friday, ran out the door and was thrusting his skateboard faster than a 'vette.

As he neared the school grounds, he picked up the board and crept cautiously along to his well-underway Science class. He moved swiftly past the ceramics room and on to the lab, barely noticing his dream girl Jennifer Moore leaning against a door, finishing a cigarette. He zoomed into the classroom and made his way towards his seat.

'Walker!' bellowed Mr Bulen, the Science teacher, from

the front of the classroom. 'Have a little trouble getting started on this fine day, did we?'

'Ahh, yes sir.' he mumbled, feeling the weight of fifty-six eyes fixed upon him. 'But I'm here now, so can we get started?' he replied cheekily. The room broke into laughter as the colour of old Bulen's face turned an off-grey and he motioned him towards the Principal's office.

When he walked in the office, he felt the warm smile of Miss Collins.

'What can we do for you today, Jeffery?' she asked, with a raised eyebrow.

'I'm here to see Mr Green, but if he's not here, I'll come back another time.' he said and about-faced for the door.

'Come in and join me, Jeff.' came a voice from Green's office. Jeff walked in and was offered a seat.

'Jeff, Jeff, Jeff.' he said, his voice taking on a desperate tone. Although he'd only joined the school that year, his pleasant demeanour was a welcome change from that of his predecessor and Mr Green was well-liked among the students. He was a tall man with arched shoulders and wore a beige suit - every day of the week! His voice was soft, and he wore wire-rimmed granny glasses. He scratched his chin as he continued, 'How many visits is this now?'

'I've lost count, sir.' Walker replied, beginning to get bored with the conversation.

'Seven. This is your seventh visit this year.' said Green as the lines on his forehead all rose at once. 'Last chance.' he said as a blue detention slip slid into Jeff's outspread hand. He shuffled awkwardly past Miss Collins, who gave him a wide smile and a wink. Embarrassed, he closed the door and headed back for the remainder of Bulen's lecture.

Upon re-joining the class, Jeff was greeted with a large piece of clay that slapped hard into the side of his face. The pain was instant, and his ear was ringing.

'Who threw that?' asked Bulen, 'Whoever threw that, please stand up!' he demanded again. Jeff was furious and stormed over to where fellow-classmate Dave Pender was sitting. Pender stood up to greet him with a fearless expression, as his 'gang' sitting around him gave their 'leader' loyal support.

'I was testing my clay pigeon Jeeeeeffffeee'….but before he could finish his smart remark, Walker's clenched right fist went hurtling through the air, crunching into Pender's face with great force. He watched him fall in slow motion as his large frame hit the floor with a thud. For the second time that morning, Bulen pointed Walker towards Green's office. He collected his books and with his skateboard under his arm, glanced back at Pender - by this stage sitting up and holding a tissue over a very bloody and broken nose.

'Not a bad start to the week.' he said to himself as he began the journey home at the end of the day. 'Two detentions, a parental guidance slip, loads of homework, and a sore cheek as well.'

This month promised to be one of the year's best for Jeff. The local football derby between Key Valley and Dannerville was on next Thursday, and the annual football dance was the following night.

I'd love to ask Jennifer to go with me, he thought aloud, as he kicked his board along and rolled his mind over for ideas on how to ask her. 'I'll call her tonight, yep, I'm going to do it. Got to get in first or some other weasel will.' He threw his school bag in his room and collapsed on the bed. 'Besides, I'm a good-looking dude,' he added, lightly running a hand over his cheek, trying to find a whisker or two, 'and she can only say no, right?'

'Is that you home, Jeff?' his mother's voice a delight to hear. 'Can you run to the store and pick me up a few things before dinner? Would you mind?'

He greeted her in the kitchen and took the shopping list and cash from her, hoping this would put him in good stead for when he gave her the message from Mr Green.

Marching home along the footpath with the newspaper under one arm, and bread and milk in the other, his heart skipped a beat as he watched Mr Green's old brown mini pull out of their driveway, then down the street in a cloud of exhaust.

'What's he trying to do to me?' he said aloud and raced the remaining 150 metres to the front porch. He opened the door and headed for the kitchen, trying to act as normal as possible.

'Your Principal, Mr Green, was just here to see me.' his mother said from the back room. 'It seems you've been getting into a bit of trouble Jeff.'

'Let's just say it was one of those days, Mum.' he said in a soft voice, hoping for some understanding.

'Pull up your socks young man, or you'll be spending the upcoming school dance immersed in homework.' she warned. He turned and headed for the safety of his bedroom.

'Oh, and Jeff.' his mother called as he swung around and faced her, but she didn't finish. Her aged face broke into a worried smile and he knew what it meant. Life had not been easy for his mum since his Dad's death six years earlier.

I miss him, Jeff thought to himself, *I'm sure he watches over me constantly and I try to carry him around with me - his spirit and his attitude.*

With that thought in mind, he grabbed the White Pages on his way to the bedroom and hurriedly thumbed the pages to the letter M.

'Ah-huh.' he murmured as his finger came to a stop at the Moore residence in Lillivale. Without hesitation, he dialled the number and sat listening to the ringing tone.

'Hello,' beamed a male voice from the other end, 'hello.' he repeated. Jeff froze and could hear his heart pounding.

'Damn it.' he said and slammed the phone down in disgust. 'You're a wimp, Walker.' he cursed, then flopped on the bed feeling miserable. He closed his eyes and drifted off into a deep sleep.

'Jeffery! Do you know what the time is? You'll be late for school!' screeched his mother from the kitchen. In fifteen minutes flat, he was showered, dressed, and out the front door with a piece of toast stuffed in his mouth. He paused briefly to run back to the door and kiss his mum goodbye.

Once on the bus, Jeff sensed two things. The first was that Dave Pender and his buddies were leering from the back of the bus and hurling a few obscenities in his direction. But he was far too occupied in another incident taking place. Jennifer seemed to be involved in a deep discussion with Nick Shinton, the school nerd.

'I can't believe it.' he moaned. '*My* Jennifer being befriended by some being from outer space who was probably asking her to the dance right before my eyes!' He could take no more. The red flag had been waved in the bull's face once too often this week. He hurried to where they were sitting and leaned over.

'Hi Jennifer.' he blurted. She looked up at him. 'Sorry to interrupt, but I was wondering if you'd, ahm well I'm just wanting to ask, I mean say' perspiration was forming on his body as he tried desperately to untie his tongue. 'Will you go to the dance with me next week?'

He watched as a warm smile formed on her face.

'Yes, I'd love to.' she replied. Jeff fumbled with the collar on his shirt and let out a sigh of relief.

'Oh man, that's great!' he said. 'Thanks Jennifer, you've made my day.'

Feeling pleased with himself, he jumped off the bus when it arrived at school and headed to his homeroom. He was on top of the world and nothing was going to bring him down that day.

As Jeff listened to the dull tones of his English teacher Miss Burke rave on about the plight of the killer whale, he gazed out of the third-floor window and daydreamed. He pictured how beautiful Jennifer would look next Friday night and how they would dance the night away. He was somewhere between dancing and plotting where to go for a second date, when the almighty thud of an encyclopedia crashed down, centimetres from his ear.

'Walker! I do hope we aren't keeping you awake.' bellowed Miss Burke.

'No, Miss.' he humbly replied, remembering the look on his mum's face from yesterday.

'Well, pay attention!'

Before long, the final bell for the day had rung, and he was on the bus home.

'Jeff, call me tonight, OK?' he turned as he was about to descend and saw Jennifer smiling. He waved to her, then stood there watching the bus creep away, coughing from the exhaust fumes. What a day. As he slid his key in the front door, he noticed a folded piece of paper neatly wedged under the doormat. It read:

Jeffery, your Aunt Casey is ill, and I have gone to Ashton for a few days - Mum.

He could not believe his luck. Deep down, he hoped that his Aunt pulled through and all, but hey, let's look at the situation here: a good-looking young guy, a date with his dream girl, a weekend coming up, and the house all to himself. He felt like a man of the world.

The sun slowly fell to end a great day and the evening was a very relaxed one. Jeff was in the garage, tinkering with his Honda CR-250M when he heard the doorbell ring.

'Jeff are you there?' beamed the voice, 'Is anyone home?'

'I'm in the garage.' he shouted back. It was his neighbour Bill Frawley whom he had grown up with. They were virtually inseparable a few years back until Bill changed schools and joined Dannerville.

'How are you Walker, what's news?'

'No news,' answered Jeff, 'school, school, and more school.'

'Well I have some big news. I've got front-row tickets for the Flame concert next month!' Bill scoffed. Jeff's eyes widened and he looked up.

'Get outta here, no way.' replied Jeff, trying to sound excited for his friend, but darn envious it wasn't him.

'Yeah, Janie and I camped overnight at the ticket office to get 'em, can't wait.' As Bill continued to dominate the conversation about himself, his girlfriend Janie, Flash from Flame's new guitar and the band's new stage show, Jeff was becoming less tolerant of his childhood buddy.

'I just dropped in to borrow your Dad's tent. Me and my old man are going camping at the gorge this weekend.'

'Sure, it's over there.' replied Jeff, pointing to an old and well-used army tent, draped over the lawnmower.

'You must miss him' said Bill, whilst neatly folding the tent. Jeff stared glumly at his skinny friend. He wanted to tell him that he *did* miss his father and that he would give anything in the world to go camping with him, just like they used to.

'Yeah.' grumbled Walker as he started to put his tools away. 'Bill,' he said abruptly, 'what's the time?'

'It's twenty past nine.'

'I've got to run, pass on my regards to your folks.' said Jeff, as he hurtled over the rose bushes lining the perimeter of the garden and raced into his bedroom. 'I hope it's not too late to call.' he said, whilst dialling Jennifer's number - not even contemplating how nervous he was about phoning her the night before.

'Hello.' answered a pretty voice on the other end of the line.

'Hi Jennifer, it's me Jeff, sorry I'm late but....'

'I've been waiting for you to call,' she said, 'I've been thinking about you a lot and can't wait for next Friday night.'

Did I just hear that? he thought to himself. *This girl who I have admired for what seems like an eternity was thinking about me!* He had to say something to keep the conversation flowing. 'Hey, guess what?' he asked her. 'I've got two front-row tickets for next month's Flame concert' he exclaimed. The words were out of his mouth before he knew it.

'Oh my god, I can't believe it' she shrieked, 'Are you asking me to go?'

'Yes.' replied Jeff happily, not fully realising what he had offered, and what he did not actually have. After saying goodbye, he sat on the bed, feeling more in love than before.

He lay awake that night for some time, thinking happy thoughts and dreaming of what might lay ahead.

| 2 |

May I carry your luggage ?

For the next couple of days, Jeff racked his brain, trying to come up with a money-making scheme, which did not involve having to beg, steal or borrow. Somehow, he had to find a way to get ahold of those Flame tickets. Saturday morning was spent knocking on store windows and asking if they needed a willing helper - no such luck. The weekend flew by, and it was Sunday night before he knew it. Jeff's mum called from Ashton with the news that Aunt Casey's condition was not improving and that she would be staying over for a few more days.

'Look after yourself, stay out of mischief, get to school on time, and do your homework!' were the only words she gave him.

But he had more on his mind than homework. He spent the next three days scouring the local newspaper for a job. Although Jeff was a desperate to find work, he was positive his skills would be wasted delivering milk or collecting stray shopping trolleys. He then noticed a job advert which got his attention. He circled it and immediately phoned the number. A few minutes later he hung up the telephone and smiled,

having scored an interview the following day after school –
as a hotel porter.

The position was located at the Aaronson Hotel in the city
and this was a job which Jeff found very appealing.

'Tips, tips, and more tips.' he said to himself, as he descended from the bus in the city the next afternoon and
walked to the hotel. He tucked in his shirt, straightened his
collar, and entered the reception area. Behind the desk was a
young lady with beautiful, dark, waist-length hair. Her com-
plexion was smooth, and her eyes were bright and captivat-
ing.

'Hello Ma'am, my name is Jeff Walker and I'm here for an
interview.' he said shyly.

'Oh, you must be here for the porter position.' she replied,
somewhat surprised. 'We were expecting someone older, I
mean, what I meant was, you look, ahm a lot older than your
age I'm sure.' she finished. Blushing, she motioned him towards a large office at the end of the foyer and smiled.

'Thank you.' said Jeff, returning the smile. Barely having
time to gloat over the receptionist's ego-enlarging error, he
was greeted by two men in suits.

Alan and Sam Cusack were brothers and co-owners of the
hotel.

'Jeffery is it?' one of them questioned.

'It's Jeff, sir.' he answered confidently.

The interview lasted for just over twenty minutes, and as
he stood up to leave, Sam asked Jeff a question that was music
to his ears, 'So Jeff, when can you start?'

'Immediately.' said Jeff with a broad grin that covered his face.

'Perfect. See Miss French at reception, and she'll outfit you with your uniform and show you your roster.' Jeff thanked them both and assured them they had made the right decision. Things were starting to fall into place.

A few days of work here and I'll have enough money to buy those concert tickets from a scalper, he thought to himself. Then he remembered the reason why he was putting himself through all this - Jennifer. The thought made him smile. After four hours of on-the-job training, which included the preferred method of how to carry a guest's luggage, he was exhausted.

'How was your first day?' asked the pretty receptionist. Jeff smiled and walked over to her. He noticed the name plate on her desk.

'Great thanks Sandra. I think I'm going to enjoy working here.' he replied

'I think you will too,' she said, 'and my name is Miss French.' He nodded.

Jeff strode out from his new home of employment, still wearing his hotel uniform, and walked towards the station. He felt proud.

The moment he had located a telephone, he decided to share his good news with Jennifer and spent the next twenty minutes engrossed in conversation, oblivious to the fact that he had missed the last bus back to Key Valley. He sighed, threw his school bag over his shoulder, and started the long walk home.

The dance was now only two nights away, and Jeff was starting to feel nervous about it. He had dated a couple of girls before but had not taken anyone out in several months. He was also positive that he had been born with two left feet and was not a great dancer.

Jeff snuck out of school early the next day, taking his tuxedo to the dry cleaners, before making his way to the hotel. That evening's shift was hectic, with three busloads of tourists all arriving within his final hour of work. He called Jennifer when he got home and made plans for the next evening. He lay in bed, gazing outside the bedroom window, and studied the bright full moon nestled high above. He closed his eyes and listened as the crickets chirped happily to each other. He made a wish for the dance with Jennifer to be a success.

Friday was cloudy and grey. Dannerville had smashed Jeff's school in the local football derby the night before, but that did not dampen the enthusiasm of all those attending the fast-approaching school dance. Stopping off to collect his tux that afternoon, Jeff saw a bag snatcher knock an elderly lady to the ground, then race away with her purse. Quick thinking Walker ambushed the young assailant and held him down until police arrived.

'Well done, son.' a burly officer said as he handcuffed the thief and placed him in the back of their squad car. 'This guy's been on our radar for weeks. Can you come down to the station and fill out an eyewitness report?'

Jeff, knowing full well that he would be cutting it fine to make the dance on time replied, 'I couldn't mail you one, could I?' The officer and his partner grinned as Jeff reluctantly climbed in the front of the vehicle. After a lengthy wait at the station, followed by a brief interview, Jeff noted that the time was nearing 7:00 PM, which meant he had forty minutes to get home, change, and somehow make his way to the dance.

'Impossible.' he said aloud, feeling frustrated.

'You still here, Jeff?' questioned a voice from behind him. It was Sergeant Turner, one of the police officers who had brought him in. Jeff knew he had nothing to lose so explained his dilemma to the officer. 'Well,' replied Sergeant Turner, 'the showers are that way, and we've got a job to go to in Key Valley, so let's do it!'

Shortly after, Jeff Walker was seated in patrol car #102, dressed in a tuxedo, and being escorted to the annual school dance by Sergeants Turner and Lowe.

This can't really be happening he thought to himself, as they drove along Mountain View Road, three blocks from his school. It was exactly 7:28 PM when they pulled up at the kerb.

'That your date tonight Jeff?' Sergeant Lowe asked as they all noticed Jennifer simultaneously. She was standing alone and looked stunning in a pink satin, shoulderless dress.

'Uh, huh.' Jeff nodded, as he shook hands and thanked them both.

'She's cute.' Turner added with a cheeky smirk on his face. The police car pulled away, and Jennifer greeted Jeff with a kiss on the cheek. To hide his embarrassment, he quickly filled her in on his eventful afternoon. They joined hands and made their way to the entrance. Once inside, they headed for the punch bowl and stood smiling and laughing, enjoying each other's company.

'Walker you ol' son of a gun!' came a voice from beyond. 'I didn't know you were coming tonight.' It was Bill, who was with Janie, his girlfriend of two years.

'You didn't ask.' replied Jeff with a forced smile. Introductions over with, Jeff was keen to get away and not waste time making small talk with Bill and Janie.

'Did you know we slept out and got front-row tickets for next month's Flame show?' exclaimed Janie, aiming the news in Jennifer's direction.

'Yeah, so have we, haven't we Jeff?' answered Jennifer. Jeff cringed, turned, and helped himself to more punch, wishing it were something stronger.

'But the concert is all sold out!' retorted Bill, detecting something fishy from his boyhood buddy.

'Contacts.' said Jeff, giving the nose tap gesture. He quickly grabbed Jennifer's hand and they headed for the dance floor.

Jennifer looked gorgeous and was a terrific dancer. They made a cute couple and with the mass of students all grooving along to local band 'The Fifty-Eights' no one noticed just how awkwardly Jeff was moving. He was starting to feel the effects from the punch, no doubt spiked with booze and was twisting and turning, like a string puppet having a fit.

'This band are far out,' said Jennifer, 'I thought, because of their band name, they'd be playing songs by Chuck Berry or Eddie Cochrane.'

Jeff nodded and moved towards her ear to talk over the music. 'I heard someone say it's the year they were all born.' Jen smiled in acknowledgement and continued dancing.

The evening was going well, and after a long and sweaty spell under the mirror ball, they decided to refresh their glasses and mingle.

'Look at that guy Christine Carruthers is dancing with!' blurted Jennifer, amused at the sight of Dave Pender with his nose swathed in a white bandage. They laughed until their stomachs ached. She momentarily lost her balance, but Jeff caught her in his arms and held her close to him. Their eyes stayed fixed on each other and she gave a shy smile. They kissed. Jeff's heart was beating fast as he held Jennifer close to him.

'We'd like to turn things up now and set course for Moscow, so if you know this one, get on the floor and dance.' shouted The Fifty-Eights lead singer. The band then broke into a raucous rendition of *Back In The U.S.S.R.* by The Beatles. Jeff led his princess back to the dance floor, and unlike everyone else who were dancing in rhythm, they held each other close and danced slowly. The next couple of hours passed quickly, and the evening was coming to an end.

'What time is your Dad picking you up?' asked Jeff.

'He'll be here very soon.' replied Jennifer as they walked towards the exit arm in arm. A few minutes later, Mr Moore's brand-new Chrysler Cordoba pulled up alongside the young couple.

'Call me tomorrow.' she whispered, then gave him a warm kiss goodbye. Jeff watched Jen and her father drive away until they were gone from view.

'What a wonderful night.' he said and sighed contentedly.

He started the journey home, thinking of nothing but

Jennifer. With his hands in his trouser pockets, he merrily kicked a stone along the sidewalk, humming Flame songs as he walked.

When he arrived home the phone was ringing.

'Hello.' he answered.

'I just wanted to thank you again for a perfect evening.' beamed Jennifer from the other end of the line. He collapsed into bed exhausted, his feet weary from dancing and walking, and immediately fell asleep.

Jeff was awoken the next morning, by the sound of the ringing telephone.

'Yeah?' he answered sleepily.

'What kind of a game do you think you're playing Walker? You were meant to sign on an hour ago!' yelled the angry male voice of Sam Cusack.

'Sorry sir.' stuttered Jeff, sitting upright and awake. 'I'll be straight over.'

He ran for the bathroom sink, splashed cold water on his face and then located his unironed uniform. Noticing the time was after nine, he ripped off his shirt and hurried to find the iron in another room, stubbing his big toe on the wall in the process. He let out an almighty cry, then feverishly pressed his crumpled clothing.

He passed Mr Cusack in the hotel foyer as he rushed into work.

'Sorry I'm late sir. It won't happen again.'

Cusack, seeing the worried expression on Walker's face, gave a short smile.

'Make sure it doesn't.'

Jeff worked especially hard that day and put in an extra two hours of overtime. He spent some time after work sipping coffee and telling Miss French all about the previous evening. Miss French smiled. As she vacated the staff room she turned and said to him, 'She certainly is a lucky young lady.' then walked off.

Jeff felt embarrassed and flattered. He finished his coffee and headed to the station.

A taxi pulled away from his house as Jeff descended the bus. His mum had returned. He ran over to greet her and help with her luggage.

'Well,' she said in shock, 'I know you're pleased to see me, but you didn't have to dress for the part.' Jeff told his mum all about the new job, and how he had kept up with his studies whilst she was away. Switching the kettle on, she stared straight at her son and said, 'I'm sorry Jeff, but you'll have to quit,' adding, 'your schoolwork is far too important to neglect.'

Just as Jeff began to state his case, his weary mother, whilst stirring her cup of hot chocolate interrupted him.

'I've had a long flight and an even longer day. I'm going to bed.'

'We'll discuss it tomorrow OK?' said Jeff hopefully, as she walked down the hallway.

'There's nothing to discuss.' she replied and shut her bedroom door. Feeling frustrated that all his good work had been in vain, he could think of only one thing that would cheer him up. He picked up the phone and called Jennifer. An hour later, Jeff's head hit the pillow with a love-struck smile on his face. He was now even more determined to confront his mother on this issue and lay there thinking of ways in which he could change her mind.

The distinct clinking sound of dishes being washed woke Jeff up early on Sunday morning.

'Good morning Jeffery.' his mum said, as her only son walked wearily into the kitchen. 'Sleep well?'

'Fine thanks.' replied Jeff, intrigued by his mother's pleasant mood. She began to fry bacon and eggs, then sat down in front of him at the small table. Staring blankly at the froth spinning at the top of her coffee, she began to speak.

'I'd like to apologize for how I spoke to you last night.'

What's this? Jeff thought to himself, quickly shifting his attention from the music column to his mother's face.

'I've had some time to think about it, and providing you lift your grades at school, you can keep the job.' Jeff was elated and jumped out of his chair to give her a big hug.

'Thanks, mum, you're the greatest.'

'But we'll give it a trial run for a couple of months OK?' she further added.

'Yeah, sure thing.' Jeff replied. He began to hungrily devour his breakfast whilst telling his mother all about his new job, the school dance, and of course, Jennifer.

'I've got some news too. We've got visitors this week.' exclaimed Mrs Walker.

'Great,' said Jeff under his breath with a hint of sarcasm, 'and who might that be?'

'Aunt Casey, Uncle Jack, and your cousin Brad. The doctors advised Casey to take things easy after her operation, and she's decided that getting away from Ashton for a couple of weeks is a good idea. It must be nearly ten years since you've last seen Brad, and it'll do you good.'

Jeff was silent as he washed the breakfast dishes.

'When do they get here?' he asked unenthusiastically.

'Tuesday afternoon.' answered his mother. 'I'd like you to be at the airport with me when they arrive.'

'Ahh, I've got to work.' said Jeff, drying his hands on a dishcloth. He gave her a short smile and returned to his bedroom.

Once dressed, he walked to the garage, kick-started his Honda and headed for Mount Clifton. After churning the rugged mountain terrain for most of the morning, Jeff decided it was time to head home. He cleared his visor, then began to descend the mountain towards Key Valley.....via Lillivale - Jen's home suburb!

'What a great idea,' he said to himself, 'Jennifer will be so surprised to see me.' Turning slowly into Lincoln Place, he came to a stop outside number 84. It was a beautiful white two-story house, with a double garage and a well-manicured lawn.

Covered in dust and dirt, Jeff wheeled his trail bike to the end of the driveway. Playing alone on the front steps was Jennifer's eight-year-old brother, a cute looking kid with blonde hair, freckles, and a couple of front teeth missing.

'Hi there.' he said to the boy. 'My name's Jeff, and you must be Randy?'

The boy nodded, jumped to his feet, and raced past a bewildered Jeff screaming 'Jennifer, your boyfriend's here!' As Jeff watched Randy run to the back of the house, he noticed a curtain move from an upstairs bedroom. It was Jennifer. She smiled warmly and waved at her mud-splattered sweetheart standing below. The large white front door opened, and Jeff was greeted by Jennifer's Mum who shook his hand and invited him inside.

'We've heard an awful lot about you.' she said as Jeff placed his helmet on a chair adjacent the front door.

'All good I hope?' he replied with a grin.

'Hello son.' said Mr Moore, as he walked from the living room and gave Jeff a firm handshake. 'I forgot to thank you for looking after our little girl last Friday night.'

'Oh, it was a pleasure.' answered Jeff as he noticed Jen standing in front of him.

'Hi there stranger.' she said giving him a hug. 'This is a lovely surprise.'

'I take it you've already met Randy?' asked Mrs Moore, as her youngest child shyly entered the room.

'Sure have.' Jeff answered.

'We were just about to sit down for lunch, you're most welcome to join us.' said Mrs Moore. Jeff noticed Jen's eyes light up at this offer.

'As long as it's no trouble, I'd love to.' he answered happily. He did his best to clean up, then joined the Moore family for a delicious Sunday lunch of roast lamb. After saying grace, young Randy, who it seemed had taken a shining to the 'big brother' type guest, excitedly entertained his family with various schoolyard stories.

'My Dad's taking me to see the Blue Sox play the Tigers soon.' he shrieked.

'Cool.' replied Jeff.

'Do you go to the baseball with your Dad?' asked Randy.

'Randy!' blurted Jennifer, at her unknowing little brother.

'It's OK Jen,' said Jeff, 'really it is. My Dad passed away six years ago.' he added shrugging his shoulders.

'I'm deeply sorry.' said Mr Moore feeling embarrassed about the situation.

'It's OK' confirmed Jeff. 'It was a long time ago. Time is a good healer.'

'Maybe you can come with us.' piped Randy.

'I just might do that.' said Jeff with a smile.

Jennifer and Jeff spent most of that glorious Sunday afternoon holding hands and chatting on the swing set in her backyard.

'What a perfect way to end a weekend.' he said, before farewelling his girl and her family.

'I'll see you at school tomorrow.' said Jen, as she waved and watched Jeff ride away on his muddy Honda.

| 3 |

Relatives come to stay

The beginning of the week got off to a hectic start, with Jeff asked to do an extra night's work on Monday. He arrived home to find his mother, normally in bed by this time, frantically running over the living room with the Hoover.

'Mum,' he said, 'just what are you doing?'

'Your relatives will be here in two days and I want the place to be spotless.' she answered. 'I know we haven't got a fraction of the money they have, but I want them to find us...'

'Exactly as we always are.' he interrupted. Her shoulders dropped and she sighed. He walked over and hugged her.

Jeff boarded the school bus early next morning to find Jennifer had saved him a seat. They spent the journey engrossed in each other and discussed the upcoming English exam. Once at school, Jennifer joined her friends, and Walker headed to his first class. The second bell soon rang and old Mr Bulen, dressed in a long white lab coat, had the Science class underway.

'I want you to all turn to page seventy-four in your Junior

Science manuals.' he bellowed, standing to the left of the blackboard.

'Hey Romeo, have a good time at the dance?' grinned Jan Peters, Jeff's Science partner.

'Let's just say the evening went very well.' he whispered. Jan was a friendly girl who Jeff had a great rapport with, and he constantly laughed at her jokes.

'My, things sound serious.' she mocked with a friendly grin.

'Could be.' replied Jeff, poking her lightly in the ribs.

Knowing full well he had to lift his grades to keep his job, Jeff spent lunchtime in the library studying for next week's English exam, before being asked to leave by Mr Daubney the librarian, for eating in the area.

He left school at three and made his way towards the city. *Only a few more days work, and I will have enough money for those Flame tickets* he thought, as he entered the foyer of the Aaronson Hotel.

'Good afternoon Jeffery,' said Miss French. 'The Cusack's would like to see you.' she added, then carried on with her typing. Jeff's heart started beating faster as he walked towards their office.

I wonder what I've done wrong. Well, it was good while it lasted, he thought before knocking on the door.

'Ahh Mr Walker, please have a seat.' said Sam, as his brother Alan looked on.

'We've been contacted by a former guest who stayed here recently, a Miss Nishiura, does the name ring a bell?' the owner asked.

'Yes sir,' answered Jeff, 'I remember her. She was on a business trip from Japan.'

'Well she sent us a letter saying how polite and helpful you were. We love hearing positive feedback from former guests. Well done.' Jeff smiled and could feel himself turning red with embarrassment. 'Oh, and we'd also like to offer you a pay increase of $2.50.' Sam added.

'That's very kind of you both, thank you.' said Jeff grinning.

Still smiling as he jumped off the Key Valley bus, he hurried home and into his mum's room to tell her of his good news.

'That's wonderful Jeff, your Dad would've been immensely proud of you.'

That comment warmed the young man's heart as he slipped into bed to end a busy and rewarding day.

Mrs Walker was up early the next morning, baking cookies and raspberry slices for the arrival of her guests later that day. Jeff, still on a high from the day before, had risen early and made his way to school. Once again, he spent his free time in the library with his head buried in an English book. Just as the first bell sounded, he felt a warm kiss on the back of his neck. He spun around to see Jennifer smiling.

'Good morning Miss Moore.' he said, standing to give her a warm hug.

'Ahh you can go outside if you want to do that sort of thing.' mumbled Mr Daubney, as he looked on from behind the encyclopedias. They both broke into loud fits of laughter as Jeff gathered his things and left.

The day went by extremely fast, and Jeff was lumbered with homework from every class. Work was not much of an improvement either. Another staff member had called in sick, and Jeff found himself running in all directions. Nearly dozing off on the way home in the warm bus, he was awoken by the thought of his chirpy relatives at home, waiting to greet him.

No point putting off the inevitable, he thought, sliding his key in the front door.

'This must be him now.' he heard Aunt Casey say as he pushed the door open.

'Hi there Aunt Casey.'

'It's been a long time.' piped her husband Jack, standing to shake his nephew's hand.

'How are you, Uncle Jack?'

'Fine Jeffery. Hey Brad, come out here and meet your cousin.' he yelled. Jeff closed the door behind him then turned to greet his cousin Brad.

'Walker,' a loud voice said, 'it's been a while.' The two boys shook hands.

'Indeed, it has.' said Jeff.

'How was work today dear?' asked Aunt Casey, as Jeff helped himself to a cola from the refrigerator. 'Your mum's told us all about it.'

Jeff, pleased at his mother's interest answered, 'busy, but I love it.'

'You must be getting paid peanuts.' blurted Brad, munching on a cookie.

'A job's a job,' retorted Jeff, 'that's what my Dad always said.'

Trying to overlook his cousin's snide remark, Jeff changed the topic of conversation.

'So how are you feeling after your operation, Aunt Casey?'

'Fine, and I'm looking forward to getting plenty of R & R over the next couple of weeks.'

'Well, I hope you do.' said Jeff yawning. 'I think I might turn in for the night.'

'Goodnight son' they all replied.

'Oh Jeff, before you go,' said his mum, 'there was a call for you a little while back.'

'Who was it?'

'I don't know I was out; Brad took the call.' Jeff looked over to see a smug look etched on his cousin's face.

'Some girl named Jennifer, she didn't leave a message, but she sounded awful pretty and I'll have to make sure I meet her.' said Brad grinning.

Jeff groaned, then staggered to his bedroom. Upon switching on the light, he was greeted with the sight of a ready-made fold-up bed, sitting in the middle of his room.

'That's all I need.' he grumbled, wondering how long his patience would hold out. This was not the first time they had bunked together. Brad was six months older than Jeff, and they had spent a couple of Christmases together, many years ago when the Walkers had travelled to Ashton for the holiday season. The current Brad was vastly different from the skinny, seven-year-old kid Jeff had once known. Now sporting a short-cropped head of jet-black hair with matching sideburns, he had developed into a sturdily built, high school football hero. Standing close to the mirror, Jeff searched his face for any trace of whiskers. Nothing.

Whatever, he thought, shrugging his shoulders. He hit the lights then fell asleep.

At 5:30 AM the following morning, Jeff was awoken by the panting and straining of Brad, feverishly finishing two hundred push-ups. Upon seeing his sleepy cousins' eye open, Brad jumped up and greeted him.

'Come on Walker let's go for a jog.' Hoping that this was a bad dream, Jeff rolled over and began to drift back to sleep. 'I'm serious,' said Brad again, 'let's go!'

Jeff, now starting to awaken and feeling annoyed, answered, 'You can run to the moon and back for all I care, just do it quietly!'

With that, Brad promptly left the room and headed for the sidewalk, leaving Jeff to concentrate on one of his most favourite past times, sleeping.

He arose shortly after and headed to school early, not to catch up on his studies, but to avoid his all-star cousin returning from his run. It also gave him the chance to put a brilliant plan into action. Knowing Jennifer would be arriving at school well after him, he searched out a couple of her best friends.

'Hi Susan, how are you?' he said, sitting next to the long-haired blonde.

'I'm fine Jeff. Jennifer doesn't get here until 8.30.'

'That's OK.' he replied.

'Sorry I didn't get a chance to talk to you last Friday night.'

chimed her other friend, Tracey, who was sitting adjacent to him.

'No problem. The night went so fast, but we both had a great time.' he said. 'Could one of you tell me when Jennifer's birthday is?'

'Fourth of September.' answered Susan with a broad grin.

'Why?' questioned Tracey, looking puzzled.

'I've got a surprise planned. Please don't tell her I spoke to you OK?'

'Sure thing.' said both girls smiling.

Hmmn, that's only three weeks away, mused Jeff, his mind ticking over.

I'm glad I get paid tomorrow. I'll finally have enough for those goddamn tickets, and I can start to save for Jen's birthday, maybe buy her something special, he thought to himself.

'You've got to be kidding!' grumbled Jeff, as he sat down for the first class of the day.

'Attention students,' Bulen said loudly. 'I'd like you to make welcome a visitor from Ashton who will be joining us for the next two weeks. His name is Brad Delaney, please make him welcome during his short stay.' Jeff shut his eyes and clenched his teeth. 'Oh yes, he also happens to be Walker's cousin.' added Bulen, amid jeers from around the room. Brad gave a cheeky smile to Jeff as he walked past him. He strode to the back of the classroom and pulled up a chair at Dave Pender's table. Jeff put his head down and felt miserable.

'I see that side of the family missed out on the looks.' said the likeable voice of Jan Peters. Jeff turned to her and smiled.

'Thanks.' he replied, grateful for her sympathy.

'OK please turn to where we finished yesterday in your Junior Science manuals' bellowed Bulen loudly, 'Brad you can share with Pender if you'd like.' Jeff groaned and wondered if the day could get any worse. However, the day passed quite quickly, much to his delight. He decided that, as payday was the following evening, he could afford to take Jennifer out and spend some much-needed time together. He eagerly searched for her on the afternoon bus, but she was not on board.

'Do you know where Jen is?' he asked Laura Baker, who was in her Mathematics class.

'She was put on detention and had to stay late' answered Laura, keen to continue reading her trashy novel.

'Detention?' questioned Jeff in disbelief. 'What for?'

Lowering her book once more Laura answered, 'I don't know, she was joking around with some new guy.' Jeff felt his body go tense.

'This new guy, his name wouldn't happen to be Brad by any chance?'

'Yeah, that's him' blurted Laura, 'Brad Delaney from...'

'Ashton' interrupted Jeff with a sour expression on his face. He was furious. 'Thanks Laura.' He stood up and returned to his seat.

He stormed off the bus and into his home.

'Mum!' he hollered 'WHERE ARE YOU?'

'Don't shout Jeff, the whole of Key Valley can hear you.'

said his mother, who was in the kitchen peeling potatoes with Casey.

'You didn't tell me Brad was going to my school!' he shouted.

'I didn't think it was so important. Why, is there a problem?' she asked, watching him pace around the kitchen floor.

'No, of course not!' he answered sarcastically, just as Brad entered the house.

'Brad!' said Uncle Jack, 'come in here will you.'

'Howdy y'all' Brad said grinning. 'Great little school you've got there Walker.'

Jeff was not amused by the comment and glared at his cousin, 'Go to hell Delaney.'

'What's up with him?' Brad asked his mother, her tranquil day now well and truly over.

'I'll tell you what the *matter* is buddy,' said Jeff, 'first of all, you wake me up at some godforsaken hour to go jogging, then I get to school and discover you're in half of my classes for two weeks, you pal around with my enemy and if that's not enough, you start flirting with my girlfriend!' finished Jeff, full of rage.

'You're imagining it.' replied Brad, as he took a glass from the dish rack and filled it with water.

'Am I?' retorted Jeff, 'whilst you're here, keep your nose out of my business.'

'Jeffery!' snapped his mother, 'that's enough, go to your room until you calm down.'

Jeff grabbed his bag, turned to Brad, and said, 'Obviously

nine years wasn't long enough.' then walked to his bedroom. He changed quickly and stormed outside to the garage.

Kick-starting his bike, he flicked the throttle and sped off, leaving an exhaust cloud behind him. His destination? Lillivale. His mind raced as he changed gears, the sound of the engine echoing across the neighbourhood. He couldn't care less if his cousin befriended Dave Pender, or if Brad attended his school, but flirting with Jennifer was crossing the line. He wanted some answers and was confident there was a reasonable explanation for all of this.

Jeff arrived at her house just as the bus carrying Jennifer pulled up at her stop.

'Hi.' she said, hurrying across the road to greet him.

'Not like you to be on detention.' he said firmly.

'I know. You didn't tell me your cousin was going to our school?'

'Well I too was spared that wonderful piece of news.' he answered.

'He's a real troublemaker.' she began. 'Would you believe he kept on pestering me, all through math class, asking me for answers?' said Jennifer.

'Somehow I would.' answered Jeff, feeling reassured.

'Want to come inside for a drink?'

'No thanks Jen, I just came over to ask if you wanted to do something tonight?'

'Oh, I'd love to' she answered eagerly, 'except I've got to study for that damn English exam next week.'

'I've got a great idea.' replied Jeff, grinning, 'we can study together.'

'Fantastic!' said Jennifer, knowing full well that they

would not be getting much study done. 'Come over at half-past seven.' she said as he mounted his bike.

'I'll be here.' said Jeff reaching over to give her a small peck on the cheek, before pulling on his helmet and heading for home.

'Where have you been?' quizzed Jeff's mum as he entered through the back door.

'Jennifer's' he answered.

'Well you're just in time for dinner.'

The mood at the dinner table was very sombre, with idle chit chat the only sound.

'What time do you think you'll be home tonight dear?' asked his mum, remembering it was a school night.

'Ahh I'm not sure, not late.' answered Jeff, as he hurriedly gulped down his mashed potato.

'Are you partying on a weeknight Jeff?' asked his Uncle with a chuckle. Jeff liked Jack and valued the time he spent with him. The feeling was mutual and since the death of Jeff's father, Jack had made the effort to show an interest in his nephew.

'Nah, got to study for an English exam at Jennifer's house.'

'What time have we got to be there?' chimed Brad

'Leave it out son.' said Jack firmly, staring at Brad.

Jeff got up hiding a smile. 'Well if you'll all excuse me I've gotta scoot.' he said, taking his plate from the table and into the kitchen.

'Hey there buddy.' said Jeff, upon seeing Randy when he arrived at the Moore residence.

'Hi Jeff.' quipped the little blonde kid with excitement. 'I'll get my sister' he replied, before tearing up the flight of stairs to Jennifer's room.

'Hello there Jeffery.' said Mrs Moore, lugging two bags of groceries through the front door.

'Let me help you with those.' said Jeff, putting his helmet down, then carrying the heavy bags into the kitchen.

'Thank you. Jen's Dad usually helps me with the shopping, but he's had to work late tonight. What are you two kids studying for?' asked Mrs Moore, just as Jennifer appeared.

'An English exam next week.' replied Jeff.

'Well then, I'd best let you both get started. Come on down from upstairs Randy and let them have some peace.' she added

Randy reluctantly strode down the staircase, his arms crossed in disapproval.

'My folks really like you.' said Jennifer, as they settled themselves in her room.

'I like them too.' replied Jeff with a smile.

'Hey, have you heard the new Wings album?' asked Jen, slipping a cassette into the stereo deck.

'No, I haven't, is it any good?'

'I really like it,' she said, adding, 'Paul was my Mum's favourite Beatle. She actually saw them in concert back in 1964.'

'That's cool.' said Jeff. The music rolled on and so did the hours, with not a single textbook opened.

'Oh man, look at the time!' shrieked Jeff, noticing it was nearly midnight.

'We've been sitting here all this time.' added Jennifer, as she laughed and then yawned.

'I'll see you at school tomorrow.' he said as they stood and embraced. They crept to the front door and he gave her a departing kiss.

'You're really cute.' she whispered. Jeff smiled and quietly exited the house.

Jennifer waved as he pushed his bike as far up the hill as possible then kick-started it, so as not to wake Jen's parents.

A short while later, he walked into his bedroom and was greeted with the sight of Brad asleep in his bed, snoring the house down!

This guy has no shame, thought Jeff, as he reached over and yanked his cousin off the bed. Brad's body met the cold floor with a thud and Jeff quickly jumped into his warm bed. Lying motionless under his blankets, he chuckled to himself then fell asleep.

| 4 |

The Delaney's early exit

Once again, Jeff awoke to the sound of his cousin performing push-ups, but unlike the previous day, an invitation to join him for a jog was not offered. After a rushed breakfast of cereal and toast, Jeff grabbed his bag and hotel uniform then headed to the bus stop. Jennifer met him when he arrived at school.

'Hi.' she said beaming. 'Did you get home alright?'

'Fine, but there was one small problem.' replied Jeff, and he began to tell her about his snoring cousin and his rude awakening.

'That must've been funny,' she said laughing, 'hey, my Dad wants to know if you'll go with him to that ball game you were discussing the other day?'

'Sure I will, I'd love to.'

'See, I told you they like you.' said Jennifer, before heading to her first class.

The day was long and tiresome for Jeff, who was starting to feel the effects from a few recent late nights, combined with a couple of early morning starts.

Although tired, he smiled as he walked into the hotel that afternoon, with the knowledge that his first payslip would greet him at the end of his shift. As the restaurant was short-staffed, Jeff doubled as a kitchen hand that evening, washing dishes, setting tables, and peeling vegetables.

'You're doing a fine job there Jeff.' quipped Sam as he passed him.

'I think I'd better stick to carrying luggage.' replied Jeff, noting that a quarter of the carrot he was working on had been peeled away. He exited the hotel when his shift was over feeling drained, but with enough money in his pocket to get those concert tickets. He climbed on the Key Valley bus and dozed off. Waking from his brief nap, he pulled the signal cord when the bus approached his stop, descended, and trudged home.

'How was work dear?' asked mum, as he slumped onto the sofa in the living room.

'Tiring but rewarding. Where is my wonderful cousin?' he asked, as his mother switched off the television.

'He went bowling with some boys from school.' Jeff was too tired to care if Brad was out with Pender or not.

'I'm going to bed.' he said, struggling from the sofa.

'Sleep well Jeff.' said his mother, and gave him a warm embrace.

'I'll try.' he replied with a sleepy grin. 'I know Brad will, he's a snoring machine.' he added, as he walked to his room. He lay in bed awake for a few minutes, pondering about the week just passed.

He cast his mind back to when he and Jennifer had talked and danced the night away. Soon, he will be going to a baseball game with her Dad and her kid brother, and he *finally* had enough money to buy the Flame tickets.

It's been a great week, he thought, before shutting his eyes and falling asleep. The glow of the full moon shone through his window, lighting up his bedroom. It illuminated the posters that were tacked on his wall, along with Brad's clothing which was strewn on the floor.

The early morning silence was shattered just before 3:00 AM when Uncle Jack's hollers woke Jeff up.

'Quick, call an ambulance, we need an ambulance!' Jack shrieked and dashed from the room in which they were sleeping to the telephone.

'What is it?' cried Jeff, racing from his room.

'It's Casey, I think she's unconscious.' Jeff hurried to the bedroom, where his mother was holding her sister's hand. Jeff had some first aid skills, acquired from his days as a boy scout. He leaned over and checked his Aunt.

'She's got a pulse and she's breathing.' he said, as his Uncle re-entered the room.

In a few short minutes Casey was aboard an ambulance, accompanied by Jack, and on her way to Dannerville Hospital.

'You'd better go wake Brad.' said Jeff's mum, hurriedly putting on a coat. 'I'll go start the car.' she added with a grim expression on her face. Jeff and Brad flew from the house and into the car, and they drove quickly to the hospital.

It was 7:00 AM before the worried relatives received any news.

'She's fine.' said Jack, walking towards the three of them in the waiting room. 'She is awake and resting. The doctor said her blood pressure was extremely low. They were asking me lots of questions about her recent operation. She's flying back to Ashton later today for some more tests, so it looks as though our visit will be cut short' he added, then hugged his son and sister in law.

'Are you sure Casey's strong enough to fly?' asked her concerned sister.

'Yes, I asked the doctor.' replied Jack. 'He said that she is regaining her strength and will be fine to fly home this afternoon.'

They entered the emergency ward and checked on Aunt Casey before returning home. Jeff, Jack, and Brad rested in the living room as Mrs Walker served up a breakfast of pancakes and hot chocolate. After catching up on some much-needed sleep, Jack and Brad packed their bags before returning to the hospital with Jeff and his mum. Casey did appear stronger yet remained quiet on the drive to the airport.

'Take care of yourselves and keep me informed of any news.' said Mrs Walker, gently embracing her sister.

'All the best Jeff,' said Jack, 'you could write to me every so often, I'd like that.' he added.

'I'll do that.' replied Jeff, as they shook hands.

'Take care Walker.' said Brad as he too extended his arm.

'Yeah, it's been real...interesting.' replied Jeff.

A boarding call for all passengers boomed from the speakers and they waved goodbye.

Jeff and his mum stood in silence at the observation deck and watched the 707 soar high in the sky.

'Let's go home.' she said, putting her arm around her son.

Jeff spent the rest of that afternoon asleep before he was awoken by a knock at the front door. He opened it wearily to see Jennifer's smiling face beaming at him.

'Wow,' he blurted, 'aren't you a sight for sore eyes. I thought you were going horse riding this afternoon?' Deep down, he felt slightly embarrassed that the tiny house he and his mum called home, was a far cry from the delicate green lawns and double-storey dwellings found in Lillivale. 'Come in.' he said, as Jennifer wiped her shoes on the 'welcome' doormat.

'I haven't come at a bad time, have I?' she asked, noting Jeff's weariness.

'Who is that?' asked his mother, awoken from her nap.

'It's Jennifer.' replied Jeff. His mother quickly straightened her clothing and put her slippers on.

'Hello Jennifer, I'm pleased to meet you.'

'Good afternoon Mrs Walker.' replied Jennifer.

'No, please call me Barbara.' replied Jeff's mum. A new face was just what she needed to take her mind off her sick sister. 'Jeff told me all about the recent dance.'

'Oh yes, it was a wonderful evening.'

'Did he tell you about our early morning emergency?' she asked and then filled Jennifer in on the details of their early morning trip to the hospital. Jeff's mum boiled the kettle and they all sat down for a coffee break. 'Why don't we drink these outside?' suggested Mrs Walker.

'It's too nice an afternoon to spend inside.'

'I can't say I'm sad to see Brad leave.' said Jeff, sitting down at the outside table.

'At least you'll be able to sleep peacefully now.' added Jennifer, as all three of them broke into laughter.

'How are you managing your work and studies?' Mrs Walker asked her son.

'Fine. We've got an English exam this Wednesday, but I think I'm prepared for it.'

They talked until the sun had nearly died.

'I had better go and start dinner.' said Mrs Walker, standing up and walking to the back door.

'Wait, Mum,' said Jeff, 'you've had a busy time these past few days. Let me shout pizza or something.' he offered. 'You'll stay for dinner, won't you Jen?'

'Erm.' she mumbled

'Oh, go on, it'll be fun.' said Jeff's mum eagerly.

'I'd love to.' replied Jen.

'Wonderful. Let's go inside,' said Jeff, 'I'll show you my bug collection.'

'Yuck.' she replied, screwing up her face. 'I'll give that a miss.' then realising that he was only joking with her. Shortly after, they were sitting on his bed looking over some of his records and cassettes.

'Remember what you said to me a couple of nights ago? Well, you happen to be pretty cute yourself.' whispered Jeff. He leant towards her and held her close to him, giving her a long, passionate kiss.

'Are you kids hungry yet?' asked Mrs Walker, startling the young couple.

'Ahm, yeah sure Mum, very hungry.' said Jeff, a little embarrassed.

'Well it's half-past six, maybe you'd better run to the store and get dinner.'

'OK, we'll go now.' he said, collecting his wallet and putting on some shoes.

'She's cool, your Mum, I like her.' said Jennifer, as they walked hand in hand along the sidewalk.

'Yeah, she is.' agreed, Jeff.

As they returned home with the pizzas, Jeff remembered he'd wanted to buy a newspaper.

'I've just got to get a paper.' he said and darted back to the newsagent. *Great* he grumbled, upon finding the store was shut. As he walked back to meet Jennifer, he noticed a news-paper sitting on someone's front lawn. He quickly secured it and ran swiftly to catch up with his girl.

'Did you get one?' she asked.

'Sure did.' he answered grinning.

'This pizza smells great, I'm sooo hungry.' said Jennifer.

'Mmmm, me too. 'I'll race you back home.' he said excit-edly.

'You're on.' she grinned. They stood together on the street corner, about 200 metres from the Walker's driveway.

'Ready, set, go!' she screamed, and the two of them sprinted down the path laughing. Jennifer surged away and sped to the finish. Jeff was astonished.

'Where'd you learn to run so fast?'

'I used to do track meets every Saturday when I was little.' she said grinning.

'That's cool. I will challenge you again sometime when I'm

on my Honda – *and* when I'm not juggling a pizza.' Jeff said laughing.

The evening was enjoyable and the sound of Mr Moore's vehicle, pulling in the driveway ended a great afternoon.

'Will I see you tomorrow?' asked Jennifer as they stood to hug.

'Gotta work.' he replied, shaking his head.

'How are you Jeff?' asked Mr Moore.

'Fine sir. I'd like you to meet my mother Barbara.' said Jeff, motioning to his mother standing beside him.

'Pleased to meet you.' she said.

'Very nice to meet you too Barbara.' replied Mr Moore before turning to Jeff.

'Don't forget that Blue Sox-Tigers game is on next Saturday' he said, walking towards his car.

'I'm really looking forward to it.' replied Jeff.

'So is Randy.' added Mr Moore, before slamming the car door shut.

Jennifer put her head out the window and yelled, 'See you on Monday Jeff. Nice to meet you Mrs Walker, I mean Barbara.'

Jeff and his mum stood waving, then turned and headed inside. After washing the dishes, Jeff joined his mother in the living room.

'What's on TV?' he asked.

'Nothing much.' she answered, as Jeff anxiously opened *The Valley View* newspaper and located the 'for sale' column.

'Here we are.' he said aloud, noticing several adverts selling front-row tickets for the upcoming Flame concert at the

Dannerville Civic Center. Jeff circled a few ads and got up from the sofa.

'Just gotta make a couple of calls.' he said, walking towards his room. Most of the tickets had already been sold, but some guy on the other side of town had two left for $20.

'I'll take 'em.' said Jeff, pleased to track some down, but annoyed at having to pay more than double the original price for them. 'Can I come over tomorrow and pick them up?

'Sure thing.' replied the seller. 'Any time after midday.'

'Well, I've got to work tomorrow,' said Jeff, 'so I'll be over at about 6:00 PM. What's your address?'

'It's 55 Sandford Road, Winvale. My name's Col.' said the ticket seller.

'Great, thanks Col, I'll see you tomorrow.' replied Jeff and hung up the phone.

Winvale, that's about twenty minutes from where I work. I think Miss French lives in that part of town, so I might ask her if I can get a ride with her, he thought.

'Goodnight Mum.' he said, before taking a shower and going to bed.

| 5 |

An older admirer

Jeff awoke early on Sunday, excited to be finally picking up the Flame tickets later that day. He arrived at work in a cheerful mood and greeted Miss French at her desk.

'Hi Jeff, you're in bright and early this morning.'

'Yeah I wanted to catch up with you before I signed on.' he said.

'Oh yes?' she replied, raising one eyebrow.

'You live over near Winvale don't you?' he asked.

'Yes, that's the neighbouring suburb and it's quite close to where I live.'

'Well I've got to go there this evening to collect some concert tickets and I was hoping to get a ride with you.'

'Certainly,' she said grinning, 'I'm leaving at six.'

'Cool.' said Jeff and he left to grab a coffee from the machine.

'Oh, and Jeff' called Miss French. 'The name is Sandy, OK?' she said smiling.

Jeff was positive when he first started working at the hotel, she insisted on him calling her Miss French, but thought nothing of it. He scurried out to the hotel driveway to greet an elderly couple. He collected their baggage then showed them to the reception area.

The day passed quickly and at exactly 6:00 PM he went to meet Miss French.

'Are you ready?' she asked, exiting the restroom where she had let her hair down and brushed it.

'I certainly am.' answered Jeff, as they walked towards the staff car park and climbed into her shiny red Volkswagen. 'Nice car Miss French.' said Jeff, as she started it up.

'I told you to call me Sandy, all my friends call me that' she replied, then knocked a cassette into the car stereo. 'You like music?' she asked, as the sound of an electric guitar roared through the speakers. Jeff had to shout to be heard as Foreigner's *Feels Like the First Time* blasted loudly from the beetle.

'Yeah I do.' he replied. 'Who's your favourite band?'

She moved the hair from her eyes and paused for a moment.

'I love the Stones and the Beatles, Fleetwood Mac's cool too.' she added.

'Right on. Their latest album is really great.' said Jeff, somewhat surprised at seeing another side of Miss French.

'The wind's nice in your face isn't it?' she said.

'Yeah.' he agreed.

'What street are we looking for?' Sandy asked as they approached Winvale sometime later.

'Sandford Road.' replied Jeff.

'Oh, I know where that is,' she said, 'my first boyfriend lived in that street.'

'His name's not Col is it?' questioned Jeff, as they slowed the car and stopped at number 55 moments later.

'No,' she answered, 'he moved interstate a long time ago.' Jeff unbuckled his seat belt.

'I'll just be a minute.' he said and ran to the front door of the well-lit house. He returned to the car five minutes later, clutching the two concert tickets.

'What's the grin for?' inquired Sandy. Jeff told her the long and involved story.

'Wow, she must be something special.' she said.

'She is, and hey, thanks for the lift Sandy, I appreciate it.'

'No problem.' she replied.

'You can drop me at the local station if you want.' he said.

'You don't have to go home yet, do you?' said Sandy. Her face lit up as she turned to him. 'It's so boring living alone and I don't get the chance to cook for anyone. Why not join me for dinner?' she said smiling.

'Ahm I don't know.' replied Jeff

'Oh please,' she begged. 'I'll drive you home straight after, I promise.'

Jeff scratched his forehead and thought for a moment.

'Well, why not.' he answered, feeling some sympathy for her.

'It's settled then.' said Sandy grinning, as she put her foot down harder on the accelerator.

They came to a halt at a smart-looking apartment complex, then ascended four flights of stairs before entering a beautifully decorated apartment.

'Nice place you've got here.' said Jeff as he walked around the tiny living room.

'Want a drink?' she asked.

'Cola will be fine.' he replied smiling.

'No,' she chuckled, 'a *drink*,' and brought two tall wine glasses into the room, resting them on a coffee table. 'I'll be back in a minute,' she added, returning to the kitchen and placing a skillet on the stove. 'Do you eat broccoli?' she asked.

'Yeah, anything's fine.' he replied. Jeff was feeling relaxed, but slightly uncomfortable after hearing the 'pop' of a cork fly out from a wine bottle. She re-entered the living room and joined him on the sofa.

'I've got two sirloin steaks cooking.' she said, filling his glass with white wine.

Jeff, trying hard to hide his awkwardness, lifted it to his mouth and took three large gulps.

'Not bad.' he commented, coughing and spluttering.

'Don't rush,' she replied, 'let it slide down gently.' said Sandy, moving her long dark hair behind her shoulder.

'Can I put a record on?' he asked, already starting to feel a little light-headed.

'Yeah, I'd love to hear Queen. Put on *News of The World*' urged Sandy, pointing to her album rack.

'How about another glass?' asked Jeff keenly.

'Sure, help yourself.' she replied, undoing the top button of her blouse. Before long they had drunk the whole bottle, prompting Jeff to ask if there was any more.

'No more wine I'm afraid, but I do have some vodka. I'll go check on those steaks, find some orange juice and fix us another drink.' she added, kicking off her high heels.

'Not a bad idea.' said Jeff, slurring his words as he too slipped out of his shoes.

'Here we are.' said Sandy, returning to the room a few moments later. 'I think you'll like this, it's just like an orange soda.' she said giggling.

'Cool.' said Jeff. He quickly emptied the glass. 'You're right. It tastes jus, just the same Sansy.' he said. 'Can I call you Sandra?'

'You can call me whatever you like.' she said smiling, positioning herself next to him on the sofa.

'So, tell me Sanda, I mean Santa.' he said, as they burst into laughter and he fell forward. She pulled him close to her and kissed him hard. Dazed, Jeff shook his head and had a moment of clarity.

'I think something's burning.' he said, as the smell of pan-fried meat wafted through the room.

'I'll go check,' replied Sandy. 'They're fine.' she yelled from the kitchen.

'Don't worry about dinner Sandy, I'd rather be taken home,' said Jeff, adding 'I don't feel very well.' Sandy walked over to him and placed her smooth hand on his forehead.

'Maybe you'd like to stay here the night.' she asked, sliding her fingers through his shirt front.

'Ahm no thanks.' said Jeff springing to his feet, now fully aware of the situation.

'But I've prepared us a tasty dinner.' said Sandy in an alluring voice.

'Let's just forget about it.' said Jeff, putting on his shoes. 'I'll get a taxi.' he added and quickly exited the apartment.

'Wait!' said Sandy, now feeling terrible about it all. 'Let me drive you home, I'm sorry.' she yelled, putting on her shoes and running down the stairs after him. She rounded the corner to see the red tail lights of a taxi fade from view.

Sandy felt a little embarrassed about what had happened, especially after Jeff's reaction. But she did not give it another thought, knowing she would smooth it out at work tomorrow. She poured another drink and ate the sirloin steak alone.

Jeff looked a little green as he slumped across the back seat of his Key Valley-bound taxi.

'You OK buddy?' asked the concerned driver.

'I think I'm going to puke.' Jeff groaned.

'What's that?' asked the driver.

'I said I'm gonna vomit!' said Jeff, as the taxi swerved quickly to the kerb. He leaned out the window and threw up until his stomach ached. After a couple of minutes rest, the driver sped to Key Valley and pulled up outside Jeff's house. He waived the fare, glad to have his smelly passenger out of the vehicle. As the taxi drove away, the porch light at the Walker residence flickered on.

'Where the hell have you been?' asked his mother as he stumbled past her.

'You're drunk!' she exclaimed. Jeff ran quickly to the bathroom and remained there for the next thirty minutes or so.

'Care to tell me what happened?' asked his mum, as he lay down on the sofa, his head spinning.

'I got blitzed with a girl from work' he replied. 'We were drinking wine and I wasn't used to it.'

'Well, you're definitely not going back there to work if that's the kind of people they employ.' snapped his mum.

'No, it's OK,' said Jeff, 'it was my fault too; I was too naive to see what was happening.'

'Just what *did* happen Jeffery?' asked his mother, looking a little concerned.

'Nothing.' he answered.

'I've got a good mind to call this girl, right this very minute.' she said. 'A grown woman trying to seduce a boy, and getting him drunk!' muttered his mother. Jeff looked terrible and felt too nauseous to argue. He stood up, walked to his room, and collapsed on the bed - not bothering with the textbooks that were laying on top. He closed his eyes and although the room was spinning, fell asleep.

Although hungover, he woke up next morning feeling remarkably well and took a shower, the feeling of cool running water on his face completing his 'recovery.'

'How do you feel this morning?' asked his mum as he entered the kitchen.

'Not bad considering.' replied Jeff.

'That was a foolish thing you did last night,' quipped his mother. 'But I hope you've learnt something from it.'

'Yeah, I sure have,' answered Jeff with a grin, 'never mix wine with vodka.'

'This isn't funny young man. You make sure you speak to this Miss French when you get to work this afternoon OK?'

'Sure thing.' replied Jeff. 'I'd better get moving.' he added, then kissed his mum goodbye and left for school.

Standing alone at the bus stop, he reflected on what had happened the previous evening, which caused him to smile and realise how funny it all seemed in the light of a new day.

He climbed on the bus and walked towards where Jennifer was sitting, involved in a discussion with Nick Shinton.

'Move!' Jeff demanded sternly and the gangly, pimple-faced boy picked up his bag and found another seat.

'Jeffery!' said Jennifer in an annoyed tone. 'I was speaking to Nick.'

'Yes, you *were*.' replied Jeff smartly. 'Why do you talk to him anyway? The guy's a nerd.'

'He's a nice guy, with nice manners. Unlike some.' she replied, turning her head away from him.

'Jeez, I'm sorry,' said Jeff, 'I didn't mean to be rude. I have a bad migraine and I was sick last night as well.' he finished.

Jennifer, now looking concerned asked 'Are you OK? Why were you sick?'

Jeff started to tell his story, then quickly changed it, knowing it could upset her.

'It must've been something I ate.' he said, nodding his head.

The bus pulled into the school grounds and the students clambered off.

'Are you ready for the big exam this Wednesday?' Jeff asked, switching the topic of conversation.

'I think so.' answered Jen, I'll see you at lunch.'

'Oh OK,' said Jeff sensing something odd. 'Thankfully, I don't have to see Brad's face in class today.' he added, then shuffled off to his math class.

He spent the lecture doodling on a piece of paper, wondering what he would say to Sandy that afternoon. The thought of it made him tense. Jeff surmised that she was only three or four years older than him, yet her sophistication and maturity made her seem much older. Although Jen had his heart, the fact that an attractive older woman was keen on him was exciting. This was all very new to him and he was unsure how he should feel. He liked Sandy but pushed any feelings for her far away.

The morning classes passed quickly, unusual for a Monday and Jeff met Jennifer at their designated lunch area: the side entrance to the gymnasium.

'Hi.' she smiled.

'How was class this morning?' Jeff asked, giving her a tiny kiss.

'Not so bad. Tracey was telling me all about this amazing new movie she saw last Saturday.'

'Oh yeah,' mumbled Jeff, munching through a peanut butter sandwich, 'what's it called?'

'Love Letters from Heaven.' she answered.

'Interesting title.' he said. 'Do you want to go?'

'I'd love to!' she squealed. 'Tomorrow night?'

'Sure,' said Jeff, 'it's a date.

'Oh, I was hoping we could go with Susan and this new guy she's met, named Rick.' added Jennifer, whilst searching her bag for her cigarettes.

'Really?' asked Jeff, as he watched her light one up. 'You really should give them up, they're bad news.' he added, as she took a couple of puffs.

'Yeah I know, they're burning a hole in my purse.' she answered.

'Not to mention your lungs.' he replied, with a serious expression.

'Anyway, it's cool if they come along isn't it?' asked Jennifer, steering away from the lecture she sensed coming from him.

'Yeah, the more the merrier.' groaned Jeff, who was looking forward to some time alone with her. The bell soon sounded, signalling the end of lunch.

'We'd better get to class.' said Jennifer, stamping out her cigarette butt. 'Randy's looking forward to Saturday, he talks about you like a big brother.'

'Is that so?' replied Jeff, smiling. 'How cool. I'll have to take him dirt biking someday.'

'I'd rather you spend time with me than my little brother.' quipped Jennifer, playfully grabbing Jeff's arm behind his back. He swung around, held her close to him, then planted a kiss on her lips.

'You're gorgeous Miss Moore.'

'You're not too bad yourself Mr Walker.' she replied.

Jeff hurried to the station after school and just made his city-bound bus. He walked into the foyer of the hotel to see Miss French busily writing, with a telephone wedged between her shoulder and her cheek. He put his hands in his pockets and nodded, attempting to conceal his shyness.

'Be with you in a minute.' she said smiling. She hung up a few moments later and walked out from her work area.

'Sorry about last night, I feel terrible about it.' she said.

'It's OK,' replied Jeff awkwardly, 'I'm disappointed I didn't get to taste your cooking.'

'Well, maybe some other time.' she added.

A few seconds of awkward silence ticked over before Jeff broke it with a fake cough.

'Did you get home OK?' Sandy asked, as she darted to her desk to answer a call. Jeff nodded, gave her the 'thumbs-up' and then walked to the changing area.

He bumped into Max, another hotel porter who had started working at the Aaronson not long before him.

'Yo Walker, how you doin'?' asked Max

'Fine.' replied Jeff, slipping into his uniform.

'How was your weekend?' Max continued, with a cheeky grin.

'OK I guess.' said Jeff nonchalantly, sensing his colleague's curiosity.

'How's Sandy?' asked Max, bursting into laughter.

'What are you talking about?'

'Well, rumour has it that you and Miss French are erm, quite friendly.'

'What the! You're nuts and I've got work to do.' retorted Jeff. He left the changing area and upon seeing two couples waiting to check in, put on a smile and gave them a warm welcome. After whisking their luggage to their rooms, Jeff was given a generous $5 tip from each of the gentlemen.

'Cool.' he said, tucking the cash into his top pocket. 'That will take care of tomorrow night's movie.'

He ended a slow evening by watching some television and sipping down a coffee in the staff room.

'Hey stranger.' said a voice entering the room. Jeff turned to see the shapely figure of Sandy leaning against the vending machine.

'Uh hello.' he mumbled.

'Are you sure everything's OK about last night?' she asked, pulling a chair up opposite him.

'I haven't given it another thought.' lied Jeff.

'That's good. We're still friends I take it?' said Sandy, her long slender arm outstretched.

'Of course.' answered Jeff, smiling as he shook her hand.

Whilst walking to the bus station, a car honked and pulled up beside him. It was Jen's Dad.

'Need a lift son?' he said through his open window.

'I'd love one.' said Jeff happily, then jumped in and slipped the seat belt on.

'Working late?' asked Mr Moore.

'Sure am.' Jeff answered, 'You too?'

'Yeah, it never stops,' said Mr Moore, 'seems anybody with spare money lying around is investing it' he added, then turned up the radio to hear the 8 o'clock news.

'Spare money?' piped Jeff. 'What's that?'

'It's what you're gonna need if you continue to date my daughter!' quipped Mr Moore, as the two of them broke into fits of laughter.

'What's Jennifer's favourite colour?' asked Jeff, as they swung onto Mountain View Road.

'You mean you don't know?' answered her father, some-what amused. 'You must be colour-blind! What colour is her room and most of her clothes?'

'Purple.' replied Jeff.

'Correct.' said Mr Moore, still grinning as they pulled into the Walker's driveway.

'Here we are Jeff, nice chatting with you and I'll see you on Saturday.'

'I'm looking forward to it. Thanks a lot for the lift' Jeff replied, 'Oh and say a big hello to your daughter for me.'

'Will do.' said Mr Moore as he reversed from the driveway, then surged along to the end of the street.

'Hi Mum.' he said as he entered the house.

'Hi Jeff, there's a letter for you in your room, and your dinner's in the oven.' said Mrs Walker as she continued with her knitting but kept one eye on the television at the same time. Jeff threw his bag on his bed and picked up the large yellow envelope. It was from The Ashton Times, one of the country's largest newspapers. A couple of months back, Jeff had entered a poetry competition which the newspaper had ran. He dipped his hand in the envelope and pulled out a certificate for second place! The prize was an accompanying ten-dollar cheque.

'This is cool.' he said excitedly, then hurried to the living room to share the news with his mum.

'That's wonderful Jeff, I'm really proud of you.' she said. 'Can you show me what you wrote?'

'Erm, it was just some silly thing I jotted down one day; it doesn't mean anything.' he said shyly.

'Please show me.' she asked again. He handed her his prize-winning poem. She pushed her spectacles flush against her face, then lifted the entry towards the light.

'*Summer Dream,*' she commented. 'That sounds lovely.' then read Jeff's entry not once, but three times.

'That's beautiful Jeff.' she said with a proud smile. 'I wasn't aware that you wrote.'

'I'm not particularly good,' he replied, 'when I'm bored, I just sometimes write what I feel.'

'You should show Jennifer.' said his mum. 'I'm sure she'd love to see it.'

Jeff hungrily ate his dinner, then called his girl and excitedly told her of his good news. He hung up the phone, then opened his textbooks. The English exam was only two days away and he knew he needed more study. Although excited about his second placing, Jeff immersed himself in revision and was surprised to see the time had raced to 1:00 AM.

He switched off the light and fell into bed.

| 6 |

Summer Dream

A violent storm hit the local area soon after Jeff fell asleep, with many power lines brought down. Mrs Walker's first job of the day was to sweep away leaves and debris that had fallen into their yard. Jeff dozed, oblivious to it all and caught up on some much-needed sleep.

'Aren't you going to school today?' yelled a voice which shattered his tranquility.

'Huh?' grumbled Jeff, repositioning his head on the corner of his pillow, confident he was still dreaming.

'Jeff!' screeched his mother, 'It's five to nine.'

He pulled his wrist out from below the sheets and after checking his watch, quickly shot out of bed.

'I'm gonna be late.' he mumbled, as he frantically gathered some clothes and ran into the bathroom to get dressed. Knowing the next bus was not for another twenty-five min-utes, Jeff grabbed his skateboard from the corner of his room and barrelled out the back door.

'See ya Mum.' he said.

'Have a good day Jeff.' she replied, standing at the clothes-line.

'Don't forget I'm going out tonight' he added, then ran from the driveway and began to kick his board along the road.

He made good time, coasted to the school gates, and picked up the board.

'Saved.' he exclaimed, upon seeing all students and teachers gathered at a school assembly.

'I wonder what this is all about?' he mused, whilst taking cover behind a tree, awaiting the right moment to join ranks. He paused and then went for it but was caught out when his board fell from under his arm.

'Mr Walker!' boomed Principal Green through the PA system. 'Where is your school shirt?' he asked, as all eyes focused on Jeff. A few seconds of long silence passed. Jeff then noted, much to his dismay that during his chaotic exit from home, he had mistakenly slipped on a ghastly blue Hawaiian shirt! The item of clothing was no doubt a leftover from Brad's recent visit.

Jeff, sensing a laugh, decided this was too good an opportunity to miss.

'It blew away in the storm last night sir.' he bellowed back. Silence, then one, then a few and eventually most of the gathering, including teachers, broke into laughter.

'Get in my office, now!' Green hollered. Jeff trudged slowly towards the office block. He caught Jennifer's gaze from her class line, and she did not seem amused.

'Jeff, haven't seen you for a while.' grinned Miss Collins as he entered the office. 'Take a seat, he won't be long.'

Once the students had filed away to their various classes, Mr Green charged into the room with his face a dark red colour. Yet again, he was wearing that beige suit and motioned Jeff outside.

'I don't like being made a fool of Walker.' he said. 'I'm not putting you on detention, but you can spend all your recess and lunchtime picking up rubbish that was strewn about last night in the storm. Please make sure you're appropriately dressed tomorrow.'

Jeff bit his tongue and thought it best not to say anything. He groaned and cursed himself for being so foolish, then headed to his first class. True to his word Mr Green was standing outside Jeff's classroom at each meal break with a battered old silver garbage can.

Keep your country beautiful, he thought, as he began his punishment. *Oh well, at least I'll have a great night tonight.*

'You missed one.' said Dave Pender, tossing a brown lunch bag at Jeff's feet. Walker glared and chose to swim past the bait thrown by Pender and his buddies. The afternoon dragged on, and Jeff was pleased to hear the final bell for the day ring loudly. He caught up with Jennifer as she was boarding the school bus.

'Hi, I didn't see you all day.' he said.

'Yeah, I was around.' snapped Jennifer, as the bus pulled away.

'Can't wait for tonight, what time are we meeting Sue and Rick?' Jeff asked.

'7:30' replied Jennifer coldly.

'What's up?' he inquired.

'Oh c'mon, that stupid stunt with the shirt you pulled this morning.' said Jennifer.

'Oh that. It was funny, foolish but funny.' he answered grinning.

'Your antics keep getting you in trouble, why can't you see that?' she asked.

'I think you're overreacting.' he said.

'Just don't ever embarrass *me* like that. Especially when we're out in public.' said Jennifer.

Jeff was taken aback and offended by her statement. He stood up, glared at her and pulled the signal cord.

'No chance of that,' he said firmly, 'I'll keep far away so as not to embarrass you.'

The rear doors opened, and he exited the bus.

'Wait, Jeff.' he heard her say. But it was too late. He had made a mistake, paid the penalty and now his closest friend had chewed him out. Annoyed and upset, he flung his bag over his shoulder, tucked his skateboard under his arm and began the walk home. He was in no rush and took some time out in a nearby park to calm down.

When he entered the front door, the phone was ringing, and he had a fairly good idea who it would be.

'Hello.' he answered.

'Hi,' said Jennifer talking quickly, 'I owe you an apology Jeff, I didn't mean to upset you.'

'Well, you did.' he interrupted. 'I thought we have something special, that you were my best friend.' he said and there was a moment of silence.

'I am,' replied Jennifer adding, 'I've just had things on my mind, that's all and....' she stopped mid-sentence. More silence. 'I love you.' she whispered.

Jeff arrived at the cinema that evening feeling incredibly special, a feeling that he had never experienced before. It was a warm feeling that was glowing inside of him. He glanced at his watch as a cool evening breeze blew in his face.

'Hi Jeff.' said Jennifer, walking up towards him. He ran to meet her and picked her up in his arms, hugging her tight. He kissed her, then held his face next to hers for a moment, feeling her smooth warm skin pressed tight against his.

'What a welcome!' she exclaimed. 'I might have to turn around and do that again!' she said beaming. They walked into the complex and saw Susan and Rick chatting together on a sofa.

'Hi guys.' said Jennifer as she walked towards them, holding Jeff's hand.

'How are you?' asked Sue.

'Fine' they replied simultaneously, giving each other a quick, secretive look.

'Rick, I'd like you to meet my best friend Jennifer, and this is her boyfriend, Jeff.' said Sue, fumbling with the buttons on her denim jacket.

'Pleased to meet you.' said Jeff with a handshake.

'Your face looks familiar' commented Rick, 'where do you live?'

'Key Valley' answered Jeff.

'Hmmn, I know you from somewhere, but I just can't think of it.' said Rick.

'I'm sure it will come to you' interrupted Sue, as she pulled him towards the ticket booth.

They sat towards the back of the cinema and cuddled up next to each other. The movie was mediocre, yet Jeff spent most of his time with his eyes fixed on Jennifer, not the big screen. He stroked her forehead and played with her blonde hair, occasionally pausing to plant a kiss on her lips. When the movie was finished, they headed to a café next to the cinema. The two girls were busily chatting about the film when Sue suggested they all hit a disco after the coffee.

'Sugar Shack is open late on a Tuesday' she added.

'Not me thanks Sue' replied Jeff. 'I want to get home and do some more revision for the English exam and I've also got to work tomorrow.'

'Maybe another time.' said Jen.

'We can go out this Friday if you'd like?' said Rick, trying to comfort Sue a little. 'Besides, my Dad wants me to work after school tomorrow' he added.

'Where do you work?' Jeff asked, as the four friends walked towards the taxi rank.

'Valley Motorcycle Repairs, in High Street.'

'I know the store.' said Jeff.

'That's where I've seen you!' exclaimed Rick excitedly. 'You've been in for parts a few times; you own a red Honda!'

'That's right,' said Jeff, 'so, *your* Dad owns that shop?'

'Sure does. Far out! Small world ain't it?' said Rick.

'Do you ride?' asked Jeff.

'I used to race, but now I just book it around the mountain trails.'

'Cool, we'll have to go for a ride then.' said Jeff, as a taxi approached.

'For sure' replied Rick.

'Nice to meet you, Rick,' said Jennifer, as she and Jeff clambered in the taxi. 'See you tomorrow Sue.' she added.

'Where to, kids?' asked the driver.

'Lillivale, then Key Valley' Jeff replied, slipping his arm around Jennifer.

'Your phone call from this afternoon - that was the most beautiful thing anyone has ever said to me' whispered Jeff, gazing into her big blue eyes.

'I meant every word' she replied, holding his hand, then giving him a warm kiss.

'What street?' questioned the driver, a little embarrassed at disturbing the love-struck couple.

'Lincoln Place' replied Jennifer giggling. 'Number 84' she added, as they entered her street. They engaged in one further kiss.

'I love you too' Jeff whispered in her ear, as she was about to open the rear door. Jen swung around and hugged him tightly. Her eyes welled with tears. She was speechless. She got out of the vehicle and stood on the sidewalk. She waved as the taxi drove away and walked happily inside her house.

Jeff paid the driver when they arrived at his Key Valley home and included a generous tip.

'Hey thanks pal' he replied appreciatively.

'Take care now.' said Jeff, as the vehicle pulled away and he walked towards the front door. He crept through the house so as not to wake his sleeping mother.

'Did you have a nice evening?' she asked sleepily, as he fumbled about in the kitchen getting a drink.

'Fantastic,' he replied, 'I'll tell you about it tomorrow.'

'OK, I will see you in the morning.' she said.

'Goodnight.' replied Jeff, walking to his room. He sat down at his study table and opened his English books. However, his mind started to wander, and some beautiful thoughts began passing through. Noticing his second prize certificate on the table, he picked it up then proudly read over the poem he had submitted:

we watch the sun begin to die
then fall quickly from the sky
seagulls float in the summer breeze
look in my eyes, picture calm seas
a yellow moon dances in fading heat
small waves scamper then lick our feet
a soft wind plays with your golden hair
your sweet aroma compliments salt air
I clutch onto your delicate hand
and gently kiss you on the sand
just as the ocean was found by a stream
we found each other, what a beautiful dream

The next day's English exam began at 10:30. Jeff had a 'free' beforehand, which allowed him some last-minute revision time in the library. He walked into the classroom and sat close to Jennifer.

'Confident?' he murmured.

'I think so' she answered.

'OK students, you may turn over your papers now, you have ninety minutes.' said Miss Burke, peering out from over her glasses, which sat precariously on the edge of her nose. Jeff's first impressions of the exam were negative, but he remained focused and finished with a few minutes to spare.

'That's time people, pencils down,' said Miss Burke, walking around the room, 'I said pencils down!' she barked again, directed at the few individuals who hastily scrawled last-minute answers. 'I'll have your results for you sometime next week.' she added.

The students returned their exam papers to Miss Burke's desk then filed out of the room.

'How did you do?' asked Jeff, as he walked with Jennifer to the cafeteria.

'Alright, I think. That question about Shakespeare's sonnets really threw me, but everything else was cool' she answered. 'What about you?'

'I did well. I wrote a couple of strong verses for that final question. Fingers crossed I'll do OK' said Jeff. 'I have to do well in this exam to prove to myself *and* my Mum that I can combine school with work.

'Did you see Flame interviewed on TV late last night?' asked Jen changing the subject.

'No, I didn't, I was studying' replied Jeff.

'They wore scarfs and sunglasses to hide their identities. It was so cool, I can't wait to see them in concert' she added excitedly.

'Me too' mused Jeff, momentarily thinking back to his effort of securing tickets. They joined Sue and Tracey in the cafeteria and caught up on all the latest gossip.

'I'm getting another drink,' said Jennifer, 'does anyone want anything?'

'No thanks.' replied Sue. After Jen had left the table, Susan leaned over towards Jeff and handed him an envelope.

'What's this?' he asked.

'An invitation to Jennifer's surprise birthday party on Saturday week. Can you make it?' she asked.

'I wouldn't miss it for the world.' Jeff answered excitedly.

'But mum's the word.' added Tracey, as Jennifer returned with a lemonade.

The afternoon wound down and Jeff went to work in a happy mood. He was relieved to have the exam out of the way and was also excited about the upcoming party.

'I saw you out last night' commented Sandy, as he greeted her at reception.

'Really, where?' he asked.

'At the movies' she replied, adding 'What did you think of the film?'

'It was OK, I guess. Some of it was boring.'

'Was that Jennifer you were with? She's very pretty' added Sandy.

'Yes, that's Jen. You should've said hello.' said Jeff, not realising Miss French was at the screening alone and did not want to be noticed.

'I'd better continue working.' she said with a false smile.

'Howdy Max, how are you this evening?' said Jeff upon seeing his colleague.

'Walker, how you doin'?' he replied, with that same cheeky grin from a couple of days ago. 'Can you to do me a favour?

'What may that be?' Jeff answered cautiously.

'I've got to work tomorrow night, but I've made other plans. Could you please swap shifts with me?' pleaded Max.

'Hmmn' said Jeff with a serious expression. 'Now I recall a little rumour which you've been spreading around.' He paused, then smiled and chuckled. 'Yes, of course, no problem.'

'Great I won't forget this' blurted Max, adding 'You're OK Walker.'

Jeff smiled and nodded.

'Jeff can you help Miss French in reception for half an hour or so' interrupted Sam Cusack. 'She's working on a discount offer, which I want sent out by tonight.'

'Sure thing' answered Jeff.

Max, overhearing the conversation was about to open his mouth.

'Don't even say it!' said Jeff with a smile, as he tucked in his shirt and walked to reception.

'Together again' quipped Sandy with a grin.

'So, what's this task we're doing?' asked Jeff.

'Just place these two adverts in an envelope and seal it, I'll address them.' Sandy answered. She gave him a warm smile as he listened to her instructions.

'Y'know you could've come for a coffee if you'd said hello last night.' said Jeff, unexpectedly.

'Yeah well, two's company, three's a crowd' replied Sandy, before answering an incoming call. Then it dawned on Jeff that she was at the cinema alone.

'Idiot' he muttered, cursing himself.

'Have you bought any new records lately?' he asked when she was off the phone, diverting the conversation.

'Yeah I have, well not really 'new.' I found some Bad Company and Bowie albums recently at a market' she replied.

'Never heard of 'em' said Jeff, 'I do have this record at home though' he added, as Neil Young's *Heart of Gold* came over the radio. They spent over an hour chatting and stuffing envelopes.

'There, that's the last of them,' sighed Sandy, 'you'd better run these down to the post office before they close.' she said. Jeff hurried downtown and arrived just as the post office was closing - but managed to persuade the young female clerk into accepting one final delivery. He shuffled back to work and heard a car approaching with music blaring. He looked up to see Sandy driving towards him in her red beetle, on her way home. She beeped and gave him a warm smile, as the wind tugged at her hair.

| 7 |

Midnight Clouds

Jeff was busy over the next two days. He fulfilled his promise to Max, working his shift on a particularly busy Thursday evening. Friday was sports day at school, and there was to be a social game of baseball played between Jeff's class and Jennifer's class. However the ball game was cancelled due to poor weather. Not that Jeff minded, as participating in team sport was something he never really identified with.

After work that evening, he collected his pay packet and decided to visit Rick and his Dad at their bike shop. As the bus approached High Street, Jeff pulled the signal cord and disembarked.

'Hey Rick.' he said, as he strode into the shop.

'Jeff, what a surprise. How are you?'

'Fine, just on my way home from work.'

'Did you see Susan at school today?' asked Rick keenly.

'No, but I saw her a couple of days ago.' replied Jeff. 'Man, you've got some nice second-hand motorcycles in here.' he added, eyeing off a Honda CB400.

'Yeah I know,' replied Rick, 'someone just purchased that

Kawasaki Z750 over by the window. It's an awesome bike. Jeff you'll have to get a road bike in the future.'

'I'm sure hoping to. But today, I wanted to buy some chain lube.' he said.

'Sure thing.' said Rick who disappeared into a small store-room at the rear of the store.

'How much?' questioned Jeff whilst opening his pay envelope.

'It's yours, take it.' Rick replied.

'I couldn't' insisted Jeff and he placed a five-dollar bill on the counter. Rick reluctantly deposited the note into the cash register and returned Jeff his change.

'Hey, do you want to go for a burn tomorrow?' asked Rick.

'Man, I'd love to, but I can't. I'm going to see the Blue Sox play the Tigers with Jen's Dad.'

'Sounds cool.' said Rick.

'What about next Saturday?' asked Jeff.

'You're on. Cool beans' replied Rick. Jeff checked his watch.

'Catch you later.' he said, then hurried from the store and flagged down his bus.

'You're just in time.' said his mum, placing a roast chicken on the table as he entered the kitchen.

'That smells great, I'm starving.' said Jeff sitting down.

'Please go and wash your hands before dinner.' she said, motioning to the bathroom.

'I got a call from your Aunt Casey today.' she said, as Jeff returned, drying his wet hands on his shirt front.

'How is she?' he asked.

'She's out of hospital and resting at home. The doctor has

prescribed some strong medication which seems to be working. Hopefully she's on the road to recovery.'

'That's great news.' said Jeff.

'What are your plans for this weekend?' she asked.

'I'm going to the baseball tomorrow with Mr Moore and Randy, and I may do something with Jen on Sunday, I'm not sure.'

'Please be sure to clean your room sometime, it's a mess.' she said with a frown.

After Jeff had cleared the table and washed the dishes, he grabbed the phone directory and flopped onto his unmade bed. Locating the restaurant guide, he mused over the many options. This was no easy decision, as he too was planning a little surprise for Jennifer's birthday and he wanted it to be perfect.

Pippi's Seafood Restaurant. Sounds nice, he thought as he dialled the number.

'Yes, I'd like to make a reservation for two for next Friday at 7:30 PM please.'

'OK that's Friday the third, what name sir?' replied the voice.

'It's Walker, the name's Walker.' Jeff answered. He lay on his bed exhausted, placing his hands behind his head.

She'll be so surprised, he thought. With a busy day ahead, Jeff got changed and went to sleep.

He awoke at seven the next morning and immediately reached for his notepad. Some poetic phrases had entered his mind and he needed to record them before he forgot them. Jeff yawned, switched off his transistor radio and then brought his mum a cup of coffee in bed. He jumped aboard an early morning bus and headed into the city. He was on the lookout for a present for Jennifer, and with the extra cash from the prize money he had won, had narrowed his choice down to two items.

After trudging through the cosmetic sections of two department stores, he decided that French perfume was out of his price range. That left only one idea and deep down it was the one he preferred: a necklace. He gazed in the shop window of a jewellery store and that is when he saw it! A heart-shaped, amethyst gemstone on a silver chain. He eagerly entered the store and pointed it out to the shop assistant.

'How much is that?' Jeff asked, hoping it was not as expensive as it looked.

'That one's $22.95.' said the lady.

'Perfect,' said Jeff, 'I'll take it.'

'For your girlfriend is it?' she questioned, carefully slipping the necklace into a red velvet case.

'It sure is, purple's her favourite colour' replied Jeff with a grin, happy with his purchase.

He arrived home and quickly changed. At exactly 11:00 AM, Jeff answered a knock at the door. It was Randy.

'Hi Jeff, are you ready?' he asked excitedly.

'I sure am, let's go.' replied Jeff, shutting the door behind him. He greeted Jen's Dad and they set off on the ninety-minute drive to the stadium. It was a beautiful Autumn day, perfect for a long drive and great baseball weather. Randy was buzzing with excitement and could barely sit still. They arrived at the stadium and located their seats. It was a close game, with the Tigers running out winners. Late in the Tigers innings, Jack Ryan hit a huge home run, with the ball coming to rest in Jeff's hands. Randy was delighted when Jeff presented it to him, and he hugged his sister's boyfriend as tight as he could.

'Thanks Jeff, you're the best.' piped Randy with a smile.

'No problem.' replied Jeff, giving Mr Moore a wink.

They stopped off at a burger joint for dinner, then drove home.

'Can you tell Jen I'll call her in the morning?' said Jeff, quietly exiting the car so as not to wake Randy.

'Will do.' replied Mr Moore, and thanks for coming today.'

'I had a great day. Catch you later.' said Jeff as he waved goodbye. He hurried in the front door to tell his mum about the day.

'Hey Mum.' he hollered.

'Jeffery, I've got a visitor.' she replied, looking up at him from the sofa. 'Please mind your manners.'

'Sorry Mum.' he said coyly, after noticing Mrs Preston, their next-door neighbour, exit the bathroom.

'Jeffery, how nice to see you. How are things with you?' asked Mrs Preston.

'I'm doing alright, thanks.' replied Jeff. The Preston family had lived next door for over twenty-five years and old Mrs Preston was a close friend of Jeff's Mum.

She would often babysit Jeffery when he was a boy if his parents had to attend a function. He liked her and used to spend hours on weekends playing football with her sons,

Daniel and Rocky. Although a lot older than Jeff, they treated him like a younger brother. Jeff was sad when they enrolled at colleges on the other side of the country. The Preston's also had a daughter named Katie, not much older than Jeff, who was born with cerebral palsy. When she was young, she spent most of her time inside the family home, but now attended Dannerville High School.

'How's Katie?' asked Jeff

'Oh, she is fine, being her usual chirpy self. She's gone to visit her cousins for a few days.' replied Mrs Preston. Jeff made both ladies a fresh cup of coffee then sat down and told them about his day.

'I can't wait to get home and tell Arthur you caught the game ball!' said Mrs Preston. 'He watched the game on TV this afternoon.' she added.

'Is Arthur still working those long hours?' asked Mrs Walker, as Jeff yawned, excused himself then took a bath. Feeling refreshed, he grabbed a can of cola from the refriger-ator, said goodnight to his Mum and played records until late.

The sun had well and truly risen by the time Jeff opened his eyes. He sat up, ran a hand through his messy hair and stretched his arms above him.

That'll be Jennifer, he thought, as he threw on a shirt and raced to answer the ringing telephone.

'Hi Jen, how are you?'

'Missing you.' she replied.

'It's nice to hear your voice.' said Jeff.

'Thank you for giving Randy the ball yesterday, he hasn't stopped talking all morning.'

'That's OK. I'm happy he's happy,' said Jeff. 'Have you got anything planned for today?'

'What did you have in mind, Mr Walker?' she asked curiously.

'Fishing!' he said keenly. 'Let's go fishing.'

She paused briefly. 'I don't know.'

'Aw c'mon, how long is it since you've been fishing?' questioned Jeff.

'Well I….' she hesitated, 'I've never been.'

'What!' blurted Jeff loudly, waking his sleeping mother. 'I can't believe it. I'll be at your house at midday.' he chuckled, then said goodbye. He brewed some coffee and headed to the garage in search of his fishing tackle. This would also be an ideal time to share a couple of his poems with Jen.

Jeff parked his Honda in the Moore's driveway, then he and Jennifer walked hand in hand towards Lake Monohoe, which was situated south of Mount Clifton. They sat on a disused jetty, shaded by an old, creaking willow tree. Jeff gave her some instructions, then they cast their lines and settled back for a relaxing afternoon.

'My Mum packed me some fruit,' said Jen, 'you want one?' she asked, holding up a green apple.

'Yes please.' said Jeff. 'I've got something I'd like to show you.' he added, pulling two pieces of folded paper out of his shirt pocket.

'What is that?' asked Jennifer excitedly, before cuddling up close to him.

'This is the poem that won me the prize I told you about. It's called *Summer Dream*. I'd like you to read it.' he said.

The sun streamed down on Jennifer's face, making it glow as she read.

'That's beautiful.' she replied, kissing him softly on the lips.

'There's one more which I wrote the other night,' said Jeff. 'I wrote it for you.' he added.

Once again, Jennifer held the piece of paper in front of her, only this time she read aloud.

'*Midnight Clouds*' she said. 'I like that title.' then continued.

Sea breeze blows your hair in your eyes,
I move it with my hand
Alone on the beach and maybe the world,
I kiss you on the sand
Raindrops slither down your face and fall into the sea
I run my fingers through your hair and hold you close to me
Driftwood rolls onto the shore at the mercy of the tide
The incredible love I feel for you is something I'll never hide
I feel my heart beat in time with yours and smile as I realise
That all I've ever wanted from life is right before my eyes
Midnight clouds form evil shapes,
but the wind blows them away
and as I get lost in your eyes there's just three words to say -

I love you.

She reached over and leant in front of him, giving him a soft kiss.

'I love you, Jeffery Walker, I really do. This is the most beautiful thing I've ever read.' said Jennifer, as tears of happiness rolled down her cheeks.

'Jennifer!' hollered a young boy nearby. 'Jennifer, where are you?' It was Randy, who was wheeling his bicycle through the long grass near the edge of Lake Monohoe.

'That little scamp has followed us.' laughed Jennifer, breaking momentarily from Jeff's arms. 'Over here Randy.' she shouted.

'Have you caught anything?' he asked excitedly, rushing over to them.

'Nah, I guess they're not biting today.' answered Jeff, watching the young boy wind in Jennifer's line.

'No wonder!' he exclaimed. 'Your worm's been eaten, weren't you watching?' he asked. Jennifer and Jeff glanced at one another and giggled, shaking their heads.

The fishing trip was cut short when some threatening black clouds began to roll over. Randy was over the moon after landing three small bass and could hardly wait to get home with his catch.

'You coming inside for a hot drink?' asked Jennifer as they approached her home.

'Just a quick one.' answered Jeff, remembering he had to clean up his room.

'Don't tell me,' blurted Mr Moore, upon seeing his daughter enter the living room with no fish. 'The one that got away.' he added with a smirk.

'Very funny Dad.' she said.

'I think Randy fished the lake dry.' added Jeff.

'Want to stay for supper Jeff? You're most welcome.' asked Mrs Moore.

'No thanks,' he replied, 'I've got some chores to do before the weekend's over.'

Jeff kick-started his Honda and chugged through the back streets of Lillivale towards the Valley. He increased his speed to escape the rumbling black skies, which were about to unleash their fury at any moment. Light rain suddenly erupted into a thunderstorm, lashing water onto Jeff's visor and making visibility poor.

The driving rain, mixed with the fast-fading light were a dangerous combination and Jeff barely noticed a vehicle reversing from a driveway. He swerved to avoid it but was hurled onto the road as his bike slid from under him. A little dazed, he stood up slowly to inspect the damage inflicted on his Honda.

'You alright son?' asked the driver of the vehicle, rushing over to him.

'Yeah fine.' said Jeff, standing his bike upright.

'I couldn't see you with no lights on.' quipped the man, standing under an umbrella.

'You should be more careful.' snapped Jeff angrily, 'I could've been killed!'

'Is he OK?' asked the driver's wife from the front of the car.

'Just a little shaken.' her husband replied.

'Well let's go then.' she demanded, 'We'll be late.'

Jeff glared at the lady and was speechless at her attitude.

The rain streamed down Jeff's face. A flash of lightning lit the sky as he stared at the car, vanishing from view as it drove away.

'Great' he moaned, as the sting of an open leg wound started to ache. He eventually made it home and wheeled his damaged Honda into the garage.

'You're late.' said his mum as he entered the kitchen, then noticing the bloodstains on his ripped jeans. 'What happened?' she winced. 'Are you OK?'

'I fell off my bike on the way home from Jen's.'

'You'll have to get rid of that bike. It's too darn dangerous.' she said, walking him into the bathroom. Jeff went to bed soon after, with a large white bandage wrapped tightly above his left knee, and a wet cloth on his forehead to ease the minor concussion. He slept soundly and was awoken early on Monday morning by his mum.

'How do you feel this morning Jeff?'

'Alright I suppose, but I do have a headache. I think I may've had slight concussion.'

She studied the grazes along his shoulder with a worried expression on her face.

'I will fetch you an aspirin. I think you'd better stay home for a couple of days,' she said. 'Rest until you're feeling better.'

Although happy to be skipping school, the reality was that Jeff did not feel very well and was happy to comply with his mother's orders.

'Better call work and let them know I won't be going in tomorrow.' he said.

After some breakfast, he watched television, then slept until mid-afternoon.

| 8 |

Farewell Aunt Casey

He had only just awoken when he heard a knock at the front door.

'You've got a visitor Jeff.' cried his mother from the other room. It was Jen. She bounded into his room with a concerned look on her face.

'Hi.' she whispered. 'Miss Collins from the school office told me about your crash. I've been so worried about you, are you OK?'

Jeff explained in detail how his accident occurred, and she filled him in on all the day's activities at school.

'So, I hardly missed anything,' said Jeff, 'I think I'll attend part-time from now on.' he added with a smile.

'Don't forget the exam results are handed back tomorrow. I'll drop yours in after school.' said Jen. She gave him a parting kiss and a hug, then left for home. Jeff, feeling much better after seeing his girlfriend, picked up a notepad and started scrawling a few verses of poetry. The young writer soon lost all track of time and had filled in seven pages of verses before being interrupted by his mum.

'What are you writing about?' she asked, entering his room with a hot serving of spaghetti and meatballs.

'I'm trying to capture some thoughts which were on my mind. I never know when a rush of creativity will arrive, but when it does, I need to write it down.'

'You'll have to show me when it's finished' she replied with a smile. 'How was Jennifer today?'

'She's fine.' answered Jeff. 'Just worried about my health.'

'Oh, some boy named Rick called you earlier, something about bike parts.' added his mother.

'That's nice of him,' said Jeff, 'I'll call him back tomorrow.'

Just as the previous day, Jeff slept solidly, and his recovery was running smoothly.

He was awoken by a bird call early in the morning which made him smile.

Much better than the clock radio, he thought.

Jeff wrote a couple of poems then drew a few sketches, in between chatting to his mum and watching the midday movie. He was lying on the sofa, talking on the phone to Rick when Jennifer arrived.

'OK, buddy I'll see you soon.' he said, ending his conversation. He turned and gave Jennifer a hug.

'Good news or bad news?' she asked with a smirk.

'Hmmn, good news.' answered Jeff, happy to play along with her game. She pulled a piece of paper from out of her pocket and handed it to him. It was the results of the English exam. Jeff could hardly believe his eyes when he noticed it.

On the top right-hand corner in red ink was a well-earned A-He shrieked out loud and hugged Jennifer again.

'What's all the commotion about.' quipped his mum, entering the room.

'Look at this.' he exclaimed, pointing to his grade.

'Oh, that's wonderful Jeff, I'm so pleased.' she said, giving him a small peck on the cheek.

When the excitement had died down, Jeff brewed some coffee and they headed for his room.

'What was your grade Jen?'

'Well that's the bad news I was telling you about,' she said with a frown. 'I didn't do too well, and I think my parents will flip.' she replied. 'I got a C+'

'Hey that's not so bad, I've had worse than that before.' he said.

'You don't understand my parents,' said Jennifer, 'I just hope they don't ground me or anything.'

'Nah, not with your birthday coming up they won't.' said Jeff reassuringly.

'Well I hope you're right.' she said sighing and finishing her coffee.

Jen's Dad swung by on his way home from work and picked her up.

As he pulled away, Rick came screeching to a halt on the Walker's front lawn. He cut the engine on his bike, thrashed his foot at the kickstand and stood the machine upright.

'How ya doin' buddy?' Rick asked, playfully punching him on the shoulder.

'Feeling a lot better.' replied Jeff.

'Where is your bike, in the garage?' asked Rick.

'Yeah, I'll show you.' Walker replied, then led him to his battered bike.

Rick thoroughly inspected the damaged Honda for several minutes.

'The prognosis is good. How soon do you want it fixed?'

'No rush.' replied Jeff.

'Well I've got some spare parts with me and I think I'll be able to finish by about midnight,' said Rick. 'But I'll have to charge you, say half-price.' he added with a grin.

'Sounds great,' said Jeff, 'but first, let's go eat.'

Jeff introduced his friend to his mum and the three of them sat down for a quick dinner. The two boys then returned to the garage and set to work. They chatted and worked well together and eventually, at 2:15 in the morning the task was completed.

'Finally. All done.' said Rick exhausted.

'I never thought we'd finish.' yawned Jeff.

'Thanks for all your help.' he added, shaking his hand, then handing him some cash.

'No problem.' Rick replied. 'I love working with motorcycles.

'Have you seen Susan lately?' asked Jeff.

'Nah, not with all this studying she's been doing, but we'll be at Jen's surprise birthday party on Saturday.'

'How about we churn some dirt and test out the Honda earlier that morning?' Jeff asked.

'You're on.' answered Rick, as he tightened his helmet, waved farewell, and rode off into the darkness for home.

Although tired, Jeff took a shower to wash the stench of

engine oil and fuel from his body. He brushed his teeth, then collapsed into bed and quickly drifted off to sleep.

He awoke the next morning and welcomed in the first day of a brand new month, September. He felt much fitter than he had on the previous two days and eagerly made his way to school. After his recent exam score, he held his head high when he entered the classroom that morning.

'Good effort Walker.' said Miss Burke.

'Thank you.' replied Jeff, sitting down at his desk. The morning classes were boring, and Jeff was glad to see Jennifer at lunch.

'Hey, I forgot to give you this yesterday.' she said, handing him a newspaper cut out. It was an entry form from The Ashton Times, advertising another poetry competition. Yet this competition was at a national level, with the winner being awarded a scholarship at Rinder University, and an employment position writing for the Times.

'I think you should enter it,' said Jen. 'Midnight Clouds' is a wonderful poem. It made me feel very emotional and I just know it could touch the hearts of others who read it. I'm sure you could win.'

'No way,' replied Jeff, 'this competition is nationwide. There will be professional poets entering.'

'Well I hope you don't mind,' said Jennifer cautiously, 'but I kind of entered the poem on your behalf.' Jeff was silent for a moment and then smiled.

'I think you've wasted a stamp,' he said, turning towards her. 'But thank you for thinking of me. Oh by the way, would you like to see another movie this Friday night?' he asked, a cover-up for the dinner he was planning.

'I'd love to.' Jennifer replied. They smiled at one another then kissed.

'That's enough of that.' joked Susan, as she and Tracey joined them.

'Hey, I saw Rick last night.' commented Jeff.

'Really, how was he?' asked Sue.

'Tired, we were up until after 2:00 AM fixing my bike.'

'Is he coming on Saturday?' blurted Tracey. As soon as the words were out of her mouth she winced and shut her eyes, realising Jennifer was nearby.

'What's happening on Saturday?' Jennifer asked.

Fearing that their secret was out, Susan quickly answered, 'Rick and I are going to the mall with Tracey.' Jeff, Tracey, and Susan all nodded silently.

'We're going to the movies on Friday.' added Jen smiling at Jeff. She stood up and happily performed a dance move. The other three teenagers all breathed a sigh of relief.

The afternoon passed slowly, but the young couple were soon huddled together on the homeward bound bus. Jeff's mind began to wander, as he gazed out at the fast-moving scenery from the window. He was contemplating how lucky he was to be in love with a girl as special as Jennifer. He smiled, imagining the look on her face at the surprise party.

'What's so funny?' asked Jennifer curiously.

'Oh nothing.' he replied. They said goodbye and as Jeff embarked, he saw Bill Frawley walking along the sidewalk.

'Hi Bill.' he said.

'Hey Walker, I heard about your accident, you OK?'

'Yeah I'm fine, just banged up my leg and shoulder.' said Jeff. 'Come on in for a drink' he offered. The two boys crossed the street and were greeted by Jeff's Mum who was hosing the flower bed.

'Hello Bill, how's your Mum and Dad?' she asked.

'They're both fine. Dad's away on business for a few days, so it's just Mum and me at the moment.'

Bill ended up staying for dinner. He and Jeff talked about old times and chatted until half-past eight.

'I'd better get going.' said Bill.

'OK' answered Jeff, 'and I might even bump into you at the Flame concert!'

Jeff was pleased to be able to talk freely with Bill. Unlike on previous occasions, he felt no tension and it felt good to re-strengthen their friendship. After washing the dishes, Jeff read until his eyes were heavy then fell asleep.

The sound of the ringing telephone woke him at around 3:00 AM. Middle of the night calls often mean bad news, and his pulse quickened as his mum scurried from her bedroom to answer it. He listened as the tone of her voice lowered to a silent whimper and knew it was bad news. He walked out sleepily to see his mum sitting on the sofa, shaking, and weeping softly.

'What is it, Mum? What's happened?' he asked. She looked up at him as he stood in front of her.

'That was Uncle Jack.' she whispered. 'Aunt Casey died not long ago.' she blurted, then held Jeff close to her chest. 'A massive heart attack' she added.

'I'm sorry Mum.' he offered, unsure of what to say. He too

was shocked by the news, but it didn't strike him until much later. Jeff comforted his mother by holding her in his arms. After she had calmed down, he offered to make some coffee. She eventually went back to bed, but Jeff could hear her sobbing. She flew to Ashton that afternoon and helped with funeral arrangements. Jeff could not bear to witness another funeral after his Dad's ceremony a few ago and remained in Key Valley.

Although upset at the news, he decided that keeping busy was what he needed to take his mind off things. After a dull day at school, Jeff made his way to work, eager to make up for the sick day he'd taken earlier in the week.

'Hi there young man.' said Miss French. Her broad smile was a welcome tonic and instantly lifted his spirits.

'Hi Sandy, how are you?'

'Doing good.' she replied. 'How's that girlfriend of yours, you two still together?' she added with a mischievous grin.

'Jen's fine, and yes we're still together.' he answered smiling.

'Well let me know if things change.' she said, as Jeff made his way to the men's room.

As he walked out, Alan Cusack greeted him.

'Jeffery, how are you feeling after your motorcycle accident?'

'Fighting fit.' he replied.

'You're not going to need that uniform tonight.' said Mr Cusack, who then pointed to the kitchen.

'We're short-staffed again, do you mind?' he questioned.

'Not at all.' answered Jeff, relieved to be away from Sandy's area and free from her advances.

He was busy washing dishes when he heard his name being called.

'Jeff, telephone call for you.' said Sandy, standing in the doorway. He never received calls at work and knew it must be important.

'Hello.' he said

'Jeff it's Mum. Sorry to call you at work. Your Uncle Jack's not holding up too well, so I'll be staying in Ashton a while.' she said.

'For how long?' he asked.

'I'll call you and let you know when things are clearer. Love you.' she finished.

Jeff handed the phone back to Sandy with a glum expression.

'Are you OK?' she asked.

'Yeah fine,' he answered with a forced smile. 'Well, that's not quite true.' he confessed. 'My Aunt died today and it's a bit of a shock that's all.'

'I am so sorry. Would you like to talk about it over a coffee?' Sandy asked.

He could tell from the tone of her voice that she was being sincere and accepted her offer of a chat.

'I'll meet you when I finish up.' he replied.

'Good. We can sit in a café or something.' said Sandy with a reassuring smile.

The fact that his Aunt was not alive anymore was beginning to sink in. Jeff's mind was elsewhere, and he carelessly dropped two plates when he resumed his dishwashing duties.

'Everything under control Walker?' boomed Alan Cusack, storming into the kitchen.

'Yes sir.' answered Jeff, a little shaken.

'Well try to be more careful.' his boss added before abruptly walking off.

Jeff shrugged his shoulders then gave Ron the chef a half-smile before continuing. The rest of the evening was hectic, and Jeff was glad to hang up his dishcloth and meet Sandy.

'What a day.' he said, climbing into her beetle. They pulled up alongside a small café in High Street. The place was virtu-ally empty, which was odd as it was a Thursday night. After each ordering a coffee, they settled into a booth towards the back of the shop.

'So, Jeff,' said Sandy, 'what's happened?'

He told her all about his Aunt Casey and their recent visit to Key Valley. Sandy sipped on her coffee, keeping her eyes fixed firmly on Jeff's.

'You just need to take your mind off it, occupy your thoughts with other things at this time and eventually, every-thing will turn out OK.' she said.

'It isn't that easy.' he replied.

'Sure it is. You must have something in your life which makes you feel good, to take your mind off things. What about your girlfriend? You sound happy with her.'

'Oh, I am,' said Jeff with excitement. 'I'm taking her to a restaurant for her birthday tomorrow night, and we've also planned a surprise party on Saturday.'

'You see?' she said, 'you're sounding happier already.

'So I am.' he replied

'Thanks Sandy, I really appreciate having someone to talk to who understands these things.'

'What are friends for.' she said, reaching over and holding

his hand. Jeff was silent for a moment before playfully pointing his finger at her.

'Can I ask, how such an attractive woman like you, cannot have a man in her life?'

Sandy sighed whilst stirring her coffee.

'I just haven't found Mr Right yet, that's all.'

After spending over an hour in the café, Jeff paid the bill and they walked to Sandy's car.

'Thanks again for listening,' said Jeff, 'I'll see you next week.'

'Where do you think you're off to?' questioned Sandy with a playful smile. 'Get in, I'll drop you home.'

Jeff hesitated and cast his mind back to when he previously took her up on a similar offer and ended up blitzed.

'Aw c'mon,' she said, 'straight home, I promise.'

Jeff got in and they sped off down High Street.

As they turned onto Mountain View Road, Sandy suddenly switched the radio off and slowed the car down a little. The cool night breeze teased her long dark hair, which occasionally fell over her face. She turned to Jeff and stared at him, making him feel a little uncomfortable.

'I think I love you.' she whispered. His mouth fell open.

'What did you say?' said Jeff, taken aback.

'I said, I think I love you.' repeated Sandy. She flashed him a smile and they drove along the road in silence. 'It's also the name of a Partridge Family song.' she added, breaking the silence. 'I bought the forty-five when I was younger.'

Just as they turned into Jeff's street, he turned to her.

'You're a really nice person and I like you, but...'

'Save it.' said Sandy, cutting short his sentence. 'I'll see you next week.' she added abruptly. Jeff exited the vehicle feeling bewildered.

What did I do? he thought to himself.

Once inside his house, he made some toast with strawberry jam then collapsed in front of the television. Even crime fighting Kojak was no match for his weariness. Finding it hard to keep his eyes open, he drifted off to sleep.

He awoke early the next morning with the TV still on. He yawned, then slowly staggered to the bathroom and took a shower. Jeff shut his eyes tight and let the jets of water stream onto his face. Once fully awoken, he contemplated Sandy's comment last night. He felt bad about it and wanted to call her but chose not to.

| 9 |

The surprise birthday party

It had been a hectic twenty-four hours and Jeff felt relieved to be heading to school. The first class of the day was Science and the students were delighted to hear that Mr Bulen had called in sick. The celebrations, however, were cut short, when Miss Burke strode into the room to take over the class.

'I hear you did pretty well in your English exam.' said Jan, pulling a chair up to the Science bench.

'A-' replied Jeff.

'Well done.' said Jan, with a grin.

'What about you?' he whispered.

'Got something to say Walker?!' blurted Miss Burke loudly.

'No Miss.' he replied.

'Just get on with your work then.' she demanded.

Jan and Jeff spent the class passing notes, catching up on each other's news without even uttering a word.

'See ya Monday Jan.' he said, walking out at the end of class.

The morning rushed by and he met Jennifer by the gym for lunch. He immediately noticed she was in a bad mood. 'What's wrong?' he asked.

'Bad news.' she grumbled. 'Because of my mark in the English exam, my folks are making me stay in and study tonight.'

'No movie tonight then?' asked Jeff, hiding his disappointment.

'I guess not.' Jennifer replied.

After lunch, Jeff skipped the afternoon math class and snuck out of the school grounds. He located a phone booth and called Jennifer's Mum.

'Mrs Moore, it's me, Jeff.' he said quickly.

'Jeff, how are you? Or should I say, where are you?'

'Well, I've got a problem and it's rather urgent.'

'How can I help?' asked Mrs Moore.

Jeff explained to her his surprise dinner plan for that evening, and how much it meant to him. There were a few moments of silence.

'Well since you've gone to so much trouble, I guess she can go with you.' she said. Jeff punched the air in delight. 'I'll get her to wear something nice, oh and maybe you can help her with her English in the future.' added Mrs Moore.

'That is fantastic, you've made my day!' replied Jeff excitedly.

He hurried back to school and waited for the changeover of classes. He walked into Miss Burke's English class smiling. After the bell sounded to end the school day, Jeff decided to skip the bus, preferring instead to skate home.

He pulled a couple of envelopes from the letterbox and once inside his house, fixed himself a snack. He then cranked the volume on his cassette player and began to dance around excitedly. After ironing his clothes, he had a light shave, then splashed on some of his Dad's old aftershave. He was feeling good as he slid Jennifer's present into his pocket. He called a cab and arrived on her doorstep just before seven o'clock.

'Hi Jeff,' said Jennifer, 'you're a little early, aren't you?'

'That depends on where I'm going.' he replied with a grin.

'What are you talking about?'

'Don't worry, I've got it all under control.' he said.

They jumped in the back of the taxi and drove off towards the city.

'What a surprise!' shrieked Jennifer, as they stopped outside the restaurant. 'I just love seafood; how did you know?' she asked, hugging him.

'A lucky guess.' he said, grinning. The young couple were given a table with a window view. After ordering, Jeff decided that a bottle of champagne was also required to celebrate the occasion.

'How old are you son?' quipped the waiter.

'Old enough.' said Jeff, putting on a deep voice. He got up from the table and explained to the waiter that it was his girlfriend's birthday and tonight was her special night.

'I don't know.' said the waiter, scratching his chin.

'Oh, go on.' said Jeff, sliding a five-dollar note into the waiter's pocket.

'OK, just this once.' whispered the waiter.

As they ate their lobster, Jeff raised his long-stemmed glass and proposed a toast.

'To the most beautiful girl I have ever met, happy birthday, I love you.' he said.

He leant over and gave her a gentle kiss.

'I love you too.' hushed Jennifer softly.

After finishing dessert, they drank the last of the champagne and held hands.

'Close your eyes.' said Jeff. As Jennifer shut her eyes, he pulled the small, red velvet case from his pocket and placed it into her open hand.

'Oh Jeff.' she hushed. Her face lit up when she opened it. 'Thank you, it's beautiful.' She leant forward and gave him a long kiss. 'Can you put it on?' she asked.

Jeff undid the clip and slipped it around her soft neck.

'There.' he said, fastening the clip.

'I love it!' exclaimed Jennifer. 'My favourite colour as well!'

They left the restaurant arm in arm.

'What time you gotta be home?' he asked, as they clambered into the back of a cab.

'Eleven.' replied Jennifer.

'You're late.' said Jeff, noticing the time was 11:30.

'We talked so much that I lost all track of time' giggled Jennifer, nestling herself in Jeff's arms. As the taxi made its way through the suburban streets, the driver cursed under his breath, reacting to the football game on the radio.

'Thank you for a fantastic evening Mr Walker.' she whispered, as the taxi pulled into Lincoln Place. They embraced in a lasting, passionate kiss, ignoring the sighs from the irritated cab driver.

'See ya.' said Jennifer, a little tipsy.

Jeff put his arms behind his head and relaxed back in the seat, as the vehicle drove towards the Valley.

He went to bed smiling, wishing he could tell his Dad all

about his fantastic evening. So, in a quiet voice, he did just that. He sighed happily and fell asleep.

The household telephone regularly took on the role of an alarm clock and did so once more the following day. He rushed to answer it before it rang out.

'Hello.' he said sleepily.

'Jeff it's me, Rick, are we still on for that ride?'

'Yeah, but you're a bit early aren't you buddy?' moaned Jeff, before noticing the clock on the wall. It was past midday. 'Man, I didn't know it was so late. Sorry. Just come around in half an hour and we'll be off.'

'Cool, I'll see you soon.' said Rick.

Walker hastily threw on some clothes, grabbed a sandwich and headed to the garage.

He wheeled out his bike then gathered his boots, guards, and helmet, just as Rick arrived.

'Hey, Rick' he said, 'Sorry again man, I slept in.'

'That's cool, we've got plenty of time. Did you have a late one last night?' questioned Rick.

'Yeah me and Jen went out for dinner.'

'Have a good night?' asked Rick with a smirk.

'Yeah we did.' Walker replied.

They made their way slowly towards Mount Clifton and spent the next few hours churning up the terrain.

'The bike feels good.' said Jeff.

'Let's have a race and really give it a workout.' said Rick.

They mapped out a route then sat side by side.

'Go!' yelled Rick, then the two boys flicked their throttles and screeched off in a cloud of dust. Rick, displaying his racing skills, darted in front, and led most of the way. But Jeff knew the mountain a little better than Rick and overtook him on the second-last turn. He sped through the designated finish area.

'Well ridden.' said his friend.

They both jumped off their bikes and rested under a tree.

'Do you miss racing?' Jeff asked.

'Sometimes,' answered Rick, 'but I broke my leg twice in eighteen months, so that was enough for me.'

'I can't wait for tonight.' said Jeff.

'Yeah, I love parties, especially surprise ones.' agreed Rick. 'I've got to head over to Sue's house a little earlier to help set up. Jennifer doesn't suspect anything does she?'

'Not a clue.' replied Jeff, smiling. 'It's time we headed back, hey?'

'Good idea.' said Rick, as they kick-started their bikes. 'I'm gonna go the long way, via the other side of the mountain'

'OK, I'll see you tonight then.' said Jeff with a nod. He slowly descended Mount Clifton and made his way home.

Although very tempted to drop in and say hi to Jen, he decided that he would wait for the big surprise later that evening. The first thing he did when he arrived home was to call his mum in Ashton. She was still unsure of her return date but sounded a lot better than when he had last spoken to her. As Jeff had awoken late in the day, he didn't have much spare time to play with. The surprise birthday party was now a little over an hour away!

Jennifer was under the impression that she would first go to Tracey's place, and then onto Susan's house, just like many of their Saturday evenings. Jeff wanted to get there early so as not to miss anything. After a quick shower, he stood in front of the mirror, giving his hair one last comb.

'All set.' he said aloud. Once again, he called a taxi and made his way over to Susan's house in Pringle Heights.

'Jeff's here.' he heard someone shout, as he approached the front door. Rick greeted him.

'You look familiar, do you ride a dirt bike?' he asked smiling.

'How you doin'?' said Jeff, as he made his way through the large group of people.

Sue was running around frantically, making sure everything was perfect.

'Everyone here?' Jeff asked, as she rushed past him.

'Oh Jeff, good you're here.' she gasped.

'Sue, calm down and relax. Everything's going according to plan, isn't it?'

'Yes, there are about four more people still to arrive and that is it, but it's nearly time!' she replied, before darting out of the room. Jeff spotted Randy standing by the large clump of gifts, which were assembled in the corner of the living room.

'Hey buddy,' said Jeff, 'where's your Mum and Dad?'

'Hi Jeff, they're in the kitchen.'

Jeff grabbed a drink then greeted Mr and Mrs Moore.

'Good evening Jeff, I hear you had a great time last night.' said Mr Moore.

'We sure did, the lobster was delicious.'

'The pendant's lovely, it really is' added Mrs Moore. Jeff smiled as he took a sip of his punch.

'She's here!' someone shrieked, and their plan went into

action. The lights were switched off and a hush fell over the guests all gathered in the living room. Sue opened the front door and welcomed her.

'Why is it dark? asked Jen, upon entering.

'Surprise!' shouted the guests in unison, as the lights were switched on. Jennifer was speechless and hugged her two best friends. She put her hands to her face and then rushed to embrace her parents.

Tracey tapped her on the shoulder and squeezed her tight.

'Look what Jeff gave me!' said Jennifer, holding the necklace out.

'Oh, that's lovely.' said Tracey.

'Is he here?' asked Jen.

'Happy birthday angel.' said Jeff, approaching her from behind. He greeted her with a hug.

'What a surprise.' she said, feeling both embarrassed and overwhelmed.

'Happy Birthday sis.' shouted Randy, running up to cuddle her.

The drink flowed and the records played loudly as the party picked up. Jennifer was busily chatting to Jeff when he had an idea!

'Would you like to dance?' he asked Mrs Moore, as she talked to a few of the other adults there.

'Why I'd love to.' she replied. Jeff hadn't boogied since the football dance and once on the floor, really started to move and enjoy himself.

'We really like you, Jeff, you're a fine young man.' commented Mrs Moore.

'Thank you.' replied Jeff. 'You have a special daughter.'

'Yes, we know.' she said smiling.

'May I cut in?' said Jennifer.

'He's all yours.' said her mum with a grin.

'He sure is.' whispered Jen in his ear.

'Surprised?' Jeff asked, as they held each other close.

'Yes, *very* surprised. It's been the best two nights of my whole life.' she replied smiling.

'Next weekend's going to be great as well.' said Jeff, reminding her of the Flame concert.

'I can't wait.' she squealed, then spun around. 'Rick told me that you two went for a ride today. Isn't it a bit soon after your accident?' she asked, a little concerned.

'Don't worry about me. I felt fine, and anyway, I had to get back on the horse.' said Jeff, lightly touching her on the nose.

They danced and mingled with other party-goers on the makeshift dance floor, and when *Jet* by Wings blared out, the birthday girl really started to move.

'Phew I'm hot,' she said, 'let's get a drink. I'd love some champagne.' she giggled, as they headed for the punch bowl.

'Randy bought me a lovely diary for my birthday. I will be able to write down and record all the wonderful times we have together.' she said happily.

The party lasted well into the night. Susan had shared a couple of cans of beer with Tracey and they were the last couple seen dancing as the party wound down. Jeff got a lift with Jen's family.

'Is your Mum still out of town?' asked Mrs Moore.

'Yes, she is.' he answered.

'You should stay over at our house tonight, what do you think?' she said, nodding in the direction of her husband.

'Sounds like a great idea,' said Mr Moore, 'you can bunk on the sofa.'

Jeff was exhausted and not fussed where he slept.

'Thank you.' he said.

Jennifer squeezed him tight, excited at the thought of her man sleeping under the same roof as her.

Jeff said goodnight to the Moore's, then made himself comfortable on the sofa. He lay awake for some time thinking over the past few weeks, whilst staring blankly at the paintings on the wall. The wind howled through the trees outside, as the last light in the house was switched off.

'Goodnight Jeff.' he heard Jen whisper.

Jeff was awoken by the sound of Randy pushing a noisy toy robot around the living room. He yawned then scratched his head, hoping the time wasn't as early as it felt.

'Hey kiddo.' he said wearily.

'Hi Jeff.' said Randy, keen to show his guest an assortment of toys which he had brought down from upstairs.

'What time is it?' Jeff asked.

'About 6:30 I think.' replied Randy. Jeff smiled.

'I'll be back in a minute.' he said, heading to the kitchen. After downing two glasses of water, he returned to the living room and began to play with young Randy's toys. A short time later, Mr Moore came down and collected the morning newspaper from the front lawn.

'Good morning Jeff, sleep well?' he asked.

'Fine thanks.' replied Jeff, ignoring the pain in his shoulder, inflicted from the dodgy sofa.

'What are you guys up to?' he asked.

'Me and Jeff are building a city in a faraway galaxy that is controlled by evil robots!' explained Randy with excitement. Mr Moore trudged over in his slippers to inspect the progress and before long, had joined them in their early morning intergalactic activities.

'Well, well, well.' said a voice from the bottom of the staircase. 'I've seen everything now!' laughed Mrs Moore, standing next to Jennifer.

'I'll have you know, there is some very high-tech construction taking place here.' said Mr Moore with a grin. They all headed to the kitchen for a filling breakfast of porridge, followed by bacon and eggs. Jeff declined the offer of a lift home, preferring to walk instead. Not only did he burn off the breakfast, but the fresh air helped to clear his head

Once at home, he fell into bed and slept most of the day. He surfaced sometime in the evening and cooked baked beans on toast for supper.

'Mum, where are you when I need you?' he uttered, as he piled the beans onto his plate.

| 10 |

Sleeping Sea

Monday and Tuesday were uneventful, and Jeff returned home with a mountain of homework on both days. He made his way towards the hotel on Tuesday afternoon, keen to get some work done but also looking forward to getting paid later in the week.

After a hectic weekend, he hadn't had much time to think about Sandy until now. He walked apprehensively into the foyer, hoping to sneak past her unnoticed. He need not have bothered as she wasn't in that day and felt relieved as he slipped on his uniform.

'Hey Jeff, Sam the man wants you in his office, pronto!' said Max, entering the changing area.

'What's he want?' Jeff asked.

'I don't know, but he didn't sound happy.' laughed his colleague. Jeff straightened his collar then walked briskly to the manager's office.

'Mr Walker shut the door behind you please.' said his employer. Jeff could see his boss was flustered and that this was not going to be a friendly chat. He stepped out from behind his desk and paced the floor.

'Are you having a problem with Miss French?' he asked. Ten seconds of silence passed.

'No sir, why?'

'Well you may have noticed she wasn't in today. She resigned on Saturday, saying she could no longer work around you!' he finished. Jeff cast his eyes downward for a moment.

'I'm shocked.' he said, stunned.

'Well she's been with us for a long while now and we don't want to lose her.' bellowed Mr Cusack. Jeff wasn't often lost for words, but he didn't know what to say.

'Umm, I'll go and see her after work OK?' he offered.

'You do that.' said Mr Cusack angrily.

Jeff walked out of the office feeling extremely low. It was then he realised just how serious Miss French's feelings were towards him. He found it hard to keep his mind focused on the job and was pleased when his shift ended. As he trudged out of the hotel, he saw Sam Cusack getting into his car.

'I'm counting on you Jeff.' he said.

Walker ran to the station and boarded a Winvale bus. He closed his eyes and tried to think of what to say to Sandy. He found his way to her apartment block and gently tapped on her door. Sandy had just stepped out of the shower and had a towel wrapped around her.

'Jeff, what are you doing here?' she asked surprised.

'May I come in? We need to talk.' he said.

'Sure,' she said smiling, 'I'll just get dressed.'

Jeff sat down on the sofa and began flicking through a

fashion magazine. Sandy returned a few minutes later in a black silk robe.

'Drink?' she asked, pouring herself a glass of wine.

'Erm, no thanks, well maybe a small one.' he said, trying to be courteous. He watched her take another glass from a cupboard and half-fill it.

'What's this I hear that you've quit your job?' questioned Jeff, as she handed him his drink.

'It's quite simple and you already know how I feel about you.' began Sandy, 'I love you Jeff. My feelings for you are strong and I find it hard to be around you at work. Some days it's difficult to keep my mind on my job.' she finished. He paused for a moment before answering.

'I'm very flattered that you feel that way about me, but you know how I feel about Jen. Having said that, I would really like you to come back to work. I will miss you and I would hate to think you threw your job away because of me.' he said.

Sandy walked to the window, moved the curtain a little and looked outside. She turned and faced him.

'I don't know' she replied. 'It will not be easy for me.'

She remained silent and deep in thought for a couple of minutes before speaking.

'Do you think we'll be able to go out a few times for a coffee or something?' she asked.

'Sure, we will. I'd like that.' he answered with a smile.

'Answer me this question.' she asked.

'Anything.' said Jeff.

'Do you find me attractive?' asked Sandy, gliding her fingers through her freshly washed long hair.

'Very much so.' he said, finishing his wine. She smiled at him warmly then hugged him.

'You're one special guy Jeff.' she sighed. 'I'll go back to work.'

'You will? That's great news.' he said.

'Besides, we've got some pretty famous guests checking in on Thursday and I wouldn't want to miss that.'

'Really. Who is it?' Jeff asked curiously.

'Wait and see.' she replied.

They talked well into the night and the mood was relaxed. She felt comfortable with him.

'I'd better call a taxi.' said Jeff, rising to his feet.

'Why don't you stay here? The sofa's quite comfy' offered Sandy with raised eyebrows.

'I'd better not.' he replied. Sandy slumped back into the sofa feeling a little dejected. She yawned and listened as Jeff requested a taxi.

'You sure you won't change your mind?' she questioned sleepily. 'I often fall asleep here.' she said, resting her head on a cushion.

'Nah, I've got to get home in case Mum calls.' said Jeff, pulling on his jacket.

He went and stood by the window awaiting the taxi.

'I'll let myself out.' he whispered, looking over at Sandy who was gently snoring.

Jeff walked to where she was laying and placed her sweater over her. He crept out of her apartment and onto the street, just as the taxi pulled up at the kerb.

He chatted happily to the driver as they headed for Key Valley. After a hot bath, he climbed into bed and lay there thinking about Jen, Sandy and all that had happened in the past two or three months. He sat up, pulled the curtain open and gazed at the wispy clouds that had nestled around the moon. A cool wind teased the curtains and Jeff slowly drifted off to sleep.

There was a knock at the door early the next morning which woke him up.

'Oh man, who can that be?' he moaned, stumbling towards the front door. 'We don't want any.' said Jeff, before opening the front door.

'That's a nice welcome home.' said his mother sarcastically. She looked exhausted.

'Mum.' he shrieked. 'What a surprise!'

'Sorry to get you out of bed dear. I must've left my keys in Ashton.' she said, carting her baggage into her bedroom.

'How are Brad and Uncle Jack?' questioned Jeff.

'They're getting by.' she answered. 'Slowly but surely. I think the reality of Casey's passing has started to sink in' she added, making a coffee.

'What about you Mum?' Jeff asked.

'I miss her. She was the best sister a girl could have....' she paused and put her head down. 'But life must go on.' she said, stirring her beverage.

Jeff got ready for school whilst his mum went to bed and slept off her jet lag.

The day started with an unannounced visit from some Dannerville kids. A bunch of pranksters decided to greet the morning assembly with a few flying eggs. It's hard to avoid an egg-missile hurled over a wall and the perpetrators sped off in their cars. Nobody was injured. Just a few unfortunate eighth-grade students who endured the worst of the sneak attack.

'*That's gonna stink by the end of the day.*' Jeff thought to himself. A good laugh to start the day.

After sitting through Science and English lectures, Jeff's class gathered to watch the screening of an educational film titled *The World Is Yours - Go for It!* The film was aimed at students who were considering leaving school and covered possible career options. It certainly had an impact on Jeff who found it not just informative, but also inspiring. He was not sure what he wanted as a career but felt that his school days were numbered.

'Don't forget, 'Career Planning Week' starts next Monday.' said Mr Bulen as the students all filed out for lunch. 'C.P.W' as it was labelled by the students, was one whole week dedicated to exploring individual career paths. Each student would sit down with the school's guidance councillor, who would offer support. However not every student knew what path they wanted to walk down.

Jeff clawed his pocket for change, then trudged to the cafeteria. He joined his friends who were all bickering about the upcoming career week.

'Well, I think it's all a waste of time.' blurted Susan. 'I have no idea what I'm gonna do with my life!'

'She's right.' agreed Tracey. 'Some days I can't even figure out what I'm going to wear and now I'm meant to know what my career will be!'

Jeff sat quietly, munching away on a peanut butter roll.

It was as though he wasn't even there. Deep in his heart, he wanted to do something with his writing, maybe even publish a book. For a fleeting moment, as he listened to their conversation, he felt removed from his friends.

'What do you think Jeff?' asked Susan.

He took a few gulps of his cola then wiped his mouth dry.

'I think if you're unsure, stay on at school. One day you'll be given a sign and you'll know it's what you really want to do with your life.' said Jeff.

They sat looking at each other.

'That sounds very profound.' blurted Tracey as they all burst into laughter. Jeff sat there forcing a smile and half laughed along with them.

It was at that moment he was certain he did not want to spend a further two years at school. Deciding to walk home that afternoon, Jeff bumped into Bill again and was pleased to see him.

'How's school?' asked Jeff.

'Y'know, it's still there.' replied Bill with a grin. 'Hey, I heard about your Aunt. I'm sorry.'

'It's OK.' said Jeff.

'How's your Mum?' questioned Bill.

'She's coping.'

'Listen, why don't you come over to my house for a while? It's been ages and my folks would love to see you again.' asked Bill.

'Well, sure.' replied Jeff happily.

It was a pleasant afternoon and just what Jeff needed. They talked for ages, recalling past incidents and local characters whom they grew up with, and they nearly died laughing when Bill recalled how they once hurled water bombs at an old neighbour.

'His Dad opened the front door just as they exploded.' shrieked Jeff.

'I got grounded for two weeks.' blurted Bill. 'Why don't you stay for supper?' he added.

'Nah I had better go, Mum only got back this morning.' replied Jeff.

'Good to see you again.' said Bill smiling.

'Mr and Mrs Frawley said to say hello.' Jeff said to his mum, as he entered the kitchen.

'Oh, how are they?' she asked.

'Fine, they said they might stop by and see you soon.'

'That would be nice.' said his mother, taking his dinner from the oven. 'You should've called to let me know you'd be late.'

'Sorry Mum.' offered Jeff. After dinner, he quickly finished his math homework, then joined his mother in front of the television.

'Anything good on TV?' he asked.

'I'm not really watching it.' she replied. Jeff sat upright on the sofa and looked at her.

'Mum,' he said, 'I think I'll finish school after this term and try and find a job.'

She put her knitting on her lap and adjusted her glasses. 'You'll what?' she asked.

'I think I'm going to leave.' he said again. She was quiet for a moment.

'But why? Don't you want to go to college? Your Dad and I always hoped you would.'

'I think I'd like to do something with my writing, maybe one day I will publish a book of poems and I am also considering attending night school.' replied Jeff.

His Mum looked disappointed and with a sigh replied, 'I can't force you to do anything, the decision is yours. But think carefully about your future.'

Jeff smiled and headed for bed.

Wanting to prove to himself that he could write, he lay in bed and started to jot down a few verses of poetry, which he hummed through his head like song lyrics. He closed his eyes and imagined himself on a beach, overlooking a lonely girl who was crying. He called this poem, *Sleeping Sea*

Alone I sit and wonder as I gaze out to the sea
My only friend a seagull who lies watching over me
My dreams are full of memories, that are soon lost in the sand
As a little girl, my Daddy would walk and tightly hold my hand
Those days feel like yesterday and I thought they'd never end
The world can really turn on you when you haven't got a friend
A fishing boat rocks back and forth at the mercy of the tide
I'm feeling cold and very alone and it's something I can't hide
I feel so insignificant like a part of me is dying
Seagull shivers, shuts his eyes as he lies softly crying
Rainbow shines across the sky, a light rain starts to fall
The ocean is now sound asleep, I hear a distant call
Sun it streams through friendly clouds and lightens up my face

I dry my eyes and realise the future's not this place
My failures are like footprints embedded on the shore
They're washed away by rolling waves and open a new door
I feel my body fill with warmth as I lift my head above
and for the first time in my life, I feel tremendous love
The time has come for my little friend to part and say goodbye
He carries my hopes and all my dreams as he flies into the sky

Jeff's heavy eyelids fell shut and he drifted off to sleep with the notepad on his chest.

| 11 |

Flame come to town

Jeff sprang out of bed the next morning, eager to get to school then head to work. He had not forgotten what Sandy had told him. Someone famous was checking in that day.

The school day seemed to drag out forever, but at 3:00 PM, Jeff raced to the bus station and boarded a city-bound bus. After quickly changing into his uniform, he tidied up his hair and straightened his collar. He was hoping that maybe, just maybe - he would be showing someone like Farrah Fawcett to her room!

'Walker are you here yet?' boomed Sam Cusack from the foyer. Jeff scurried out into the lounge area.

'Yes sir.' he answered.

'There are people here waiting to check in,' said his boss firmly, 'and Walker, I don't know what you said, but Miss French has returned. Thankyou.' Jeff nodded before quickly showing an elderly couple to their suite.

'He's in a rotten mood.' Jeff said to Sandy as he passed her in the hallway.

'You're not wrong.' she agreed.

After a frenetic first hour, Jeff headed towards the coffee machine.

'Hey, can we get some service here please.' came a male voice from the foyer. Jeff scurried back into the foyer and his mouth dropped. Standing in front of him were the four members of Flame, with their manager and personal assistants.

'Can we check in?' asked the manager again. Jeff was frozen. All four members of the rock super-group were without their trademark face paint. Yet with their long black hair and dark sunglasses, it was easy to tell they were musicians.

'Hello.' said Sandy, entering the room. She quickly tended to the administrative arrangements and then called Jeff over. 'Can you please show our guests to rooms 211, 212, 213 and 214. Don't hesitate to call if you need anything.' she added.

Marc, the lead vocalist and rhythm guitarist, took an instant shining to Miss French and gave her a warm smile.

'Thank you.' he said in a broad accent. Jeff transported their luggage, which included a couple of guitar cases to their rooms.

'Hey Colt, how much are we going to tip this boy?' asked Flash the guitarist, to his bandmate.

'Can you break a hundred?' Colt replied, looking at Jeff. They burst into laughter and Flash winked at him.

After that joke, Jeff no longer felt numb or intimidated. The ice had thawed.

'I've got front-row tickets for your concert on Saturday.' said Jeff proudly.

'Right on.' said Flash, peering out the window. 'What's your name kid?'

'It's Jeff, Jeff Walker.' he replied.

'Well Jeff Walker, we'll get you and a friend backstage passes for the show.' said the guitarist. 'How does that sound? Just don't tell anyone where we are staying OK?'

'You got it,' replied Jeff, 'and thanks.'

'Got a favourite Flame song?' asked Colt, the band's drummer.

Jeff scratched his head and replied, 'I love *Rock 'n' Roll Cities* and also *Thrust,* that's a great tune as well.' He watched Flash undo the muselet then wrench the cork from a champagne bottle.

'Let me do that.' said Jeff, who then poured the guitarist a glass. Jeff excused himself and closed the door behind him in a state of shock.

When he arrived home, he walked into his bedroom and stared in disbelief at the Flame poster on his wall. He smiled.

'Are you OK?' questioned his mum, poking her head in his bedroom.

'I am so happy I could burst!' he replied. He wanted to tell her who he had befriended but knew he mustn't tell anybody, not even his mother. She examined him quizzingly. 'But I'm sworn to secrecy so please don't ask.' he added with a grin. She did not press him further.

After a hot meal, he went to bed. Too excited to sleep, he put Flame's *Infernum de Rock* album on his turntable and sat on the floor, reading over the album's liner notes.

The next day at school he found it extremely hard to concentrate. He met Jennifer for lunch outside the gym. She greeted him excitedly.

'Jeff, I saw Marc Vogel from Flame interviewed on TV last night!' she shrieked. 'I can't wait for Saturday night.' Jeff watched her dance around in front of him, singing the lyrics to one of their hit songs. Something twitched inside of him and he could no longer contain his secret.

'Jennifer,' he said, 'if I tell you something you've got to swear not to tell a soul.'

'Ooh, what is it?' she shrieked. 'Tell me, tell me.'

'You've got to give me your word on this.' he demanded.

'OK, I promise,' said Jennifer, 'now what is it? What's the secret?!'

Jeff took a deep breath and made certain nobody was in earshot.

'Flame are staying at the hotel and Flash said he'd get me two backstage passes.' he finished.

'Oh my god, I can't believe it!' she screamed.

'Keep it down,' said Jeff, 'I promised them I wouldn't tell anyone, and I'd probably lose my job too.' He told her all about last night and how Colt had even asked him what his favourite song was.

'I assume they were unmasked?' she quizzed. Jeff nodded. At the end of lunch, they walked towards Science class together.

'I'm gonna cut school early today and get to the hotel.' he said. 'Remember it's a BIG secret.' he added, before giving her a quick kiss on the lips. She nodded then walked to her desk in the science lab.

Forty-five minutes before school was out, Jeff made a low-key exit. He eagerly jumped on a bus and headed to work.

'Hi Sandy.' he said upon entering the hotel.

'Jeff, there's a message here for you, from Mr Fournier, Flame's manager.' she informed him. Jeff unfolded the piece of paper and quickly read it. His face lit up like a Christmas tree.

'What is it?' asked Sandy impatiently, whilst rushing to answer the ringing telephone.

'They said I'm welcome to go down and watch them rehearse today.'

Sandy muffled the mouthpiece of the phone with her hand and nodded to him.

'Jeff it's Flash from Flame on the phone, he wants to know if you can bring some Chinese food down to the Civic Center.' relayed Sandy. Jeff nodded enthusiastically.

'Tell him I'll be there ASAP.'

After she hung up, Jeff used the phone and called Jennifer who had just arrived home from school, telling her to meet him at the Civic Center as soon as she could.

'What about the Cusack's?' mused Jeff aloud.

'I'll tell them you're looking after our famous guests, which you are.' grinned Miss French.

'You're the best.' said Jeff, reaching over to kiss her on the cheek.

'Don't forget your pay packet,' she said, handing him an envelope, 'and here's some petty cash for the Chinese food. Have fun.' she added.

He hurried outside and hailed the first taxi he saw.

'Where to son?' asked the driver.

'Dannerville Civic Center.' answered Jeff. His heart started to beat faster when he heard an ad for the upcoming Flame concert over the cab's radio.

'Please stop at this restaurant for a minute.' he said, and the car pulled up outside *The Golden Dragon* Chinese Restaurant. Jeff returned ten minutes later with three large bags of food.

'Are you feeding an army?' queried the driver with a grin.

'Not quite.' answered Jeff.

As they approached the Civic Center, the loud blur of amplified guitars could be heard, which added to the excitement. A group of local kids, some in face paint, had milled outside the venue to listen to their rock 'n' roll heroes. Jennifer came rushing towards Jeff as he exited the cab.

'Follow me.' he said.

They cleared the venue's security checkpoint and once inside the venue, Jeff explained who he was to one of the band's bodyguards. He spotted Mr Fournier, who greeted Jeff with a handshake. Jennifer was speechless. So too was Jeff. The band had nearly finished their rehearsal and the two lucky teenagers were treated to three songs.

Each band member was wearing their trademark greasepaint. Marc had part of his costume on too. As they blasted through their song *Thrust,* Colt spotted Jeff and pointed his drumstick in acknowledgement. Jeff nodded and smiled. During the final song, *Dreams of Fire,* Flash ran to the microphone and shouted over the top of Marc's vocals....

'Can anyone smell Chinese food?' he asked with a cackle.

'Let's call it a day.' said T.J smiling. Colt's roadie took them backstage and Jeff introduced his girlfriend to the band.

'Can you sign this for me please?' she said, holding up a copy of their latest album.

'Sure thing.' said Marc.

'Jeff and Jennifer shared the food with the band and a couple of crew members. Jennifer told T.J that Jeff also wrote. '…mostly poems, but I think he could write songs too, if he tried.'

'Oh really?' said T.J, 'Maybe next time we come through here he could open the show for us.' said the bassist grinning.

Just then Mr Fournier re-entered and presented each of them with a backstage pass for tomorrow night's concert.

'You two wanna come back to the hotel and party?' asked Colt, washing the makeup from his face.

'I can't, my Dad's picking me up.' said Jennifer.

'That's cool.' replied the drummer. 'Jeff are you in?'

'Yeah man, I'd love to.' he said. Jennifer said goodbye and went to meet her father.

Jeff clambered into a white limousine with Colt and Flash and the car drove slowly to the Aaronson Hotel. Flash showed Jeff the vehicle's television set and opened him up a can of Ashton Ale. The teenager chugged it down. *This is too damn cool* he thought, marvelling at the technology contained in the limo.

Once in the hotel room, Flash cracked open a bottle of champagne and they cranked some music on a portable cassette player.

'This is AC/DC.' blurted the guitarist. He tossed a cassette case over to Jeff, of the band being blasted from the speakers.

'We did some shows with these cats last year. They're outta sight.'

They partied until late and Sandy, who had checked in on them after her shift, helped a drunken Jeff into her car.

'What a day!' he shouted, 'What a band! What a beautiful woman you are. You're a fox!' he said drunkenly.

'Just sit still Jeff, I'll get you home soon.' said Sandy.

'How come I had to leave the party?' he asked with slurred speech.

'Other guests were complaining about the noise.'

'You are so pretty.' said Jeff, running his fingers over her neck and through her long hair.

'You're drunk.' replied Sandy.

'No, no, I mean it.' he said again.

'Listen, I know you've had a few drinks, so don't say things you don't mean.' she said, trying to ignore his drunken remarks.

As Sandy's red beetle headed for Key Valley, Jeff hummed along loudly to a Peter Frampton song on the radio. She laughed as he tried to imitate the talk box sound effect contained in the tune. He suddenly stopped, turned to face her, then kissed her full on the lips. She swerved a little and then straightened the vehicle.

'What's that for?' she asked, bewildered.

'I just want you to know how special you are to me.' he slurred.

'Well, thank you Jeff.' she replied smiling.

Sandy's car came to a squeaky halt outside the Walker residence. Jeff got out of the vehicle, waved goodbye, then staggered towards the front door.

Fortunately, he managed to creep through the house and into his bedroom without disturbing his mother. It was late when his head hit the pillow and the alarm on his clock radio sprang to life in no time.

Feeling quite seedy, Jeff stood motionless under the shower for twenty minutes. He skipped breakfast, preferring instead to slowly sip strong coffee. Although he tried hard to hide the hangover from his mum, she was very aware of the situation.

'How was work last night?' she questioned with a smirk.

'Pretty good.' answered Jeff.

'You got in rather late didn't you?' she asked.

'Yeah, I went out with some friends.' he replied, getting up from the table to answer the phone. It was Jennifer.

'Hi Jeff, how are you feeling?'

'Not too good.' he replied.

'I still can't believe I met them!' she exclaimed, still on a high.

'Yeah, it'll be a great concert.' said Jeff.

'What are you doing today?' she asked.

'I need to clear my head. I'd also like to do some writing. Mum's got a long list of chores which need doing as well.'

'OK, I hope you feel better soon, and I'll see you tonight.' said Jen.

It was a glorious Autumn day, with not a breath of wind and the sun streamed down all day. After cleaning his bedroom and mowing the lawn, Jeff took advantage of the beautiful afternoon and sat under a shady tree in the backyard. With a pencil and paper in hand, he fine-tuned *Sleeping Sea,* occasionally pausing to lift his head and bask in the sun's rays. It was a soothing way to farewell the final remnants of last night's hangover.

| 12 |

The concert

Jeff took a shower, then changed into some jeans and his favourite denim jacket. He ate a bag of potato chips then washed them down with cola. He met Jennifer at the Civic Center, where a large crowd had already begun to fill the hall. She removed the backing from his backstage pass and pressed the satin sticker on his jacket. Before repeating the process on herself, she asked him the meaning of the 'AAA' letters, printed on the pass.

'Access All Areas.' answered Jeff excitedly. 'These are usually given out to the band members and also the promoter.'

She squealed with delight and walked proudly through the waiting crowd. You could sense the excitement in the air, as the young couple waited by the side of the stage for the show to start.

A little after 8:00 PM, the house lights dimmed and a loud voice boomed over the PA system; *Alright Dannerville – light the torch, it's time to get scorched - get on your feet and feel the rock 'n' roll heat...of FLAME!*

Lights flashed, dry ice filled the stage, pyro exploded and

the greatest rock 'n' roll show on earth had begun! The band sounded tight, as Marc screamed through the set-opener, *Rock 'n' Roll Cities*. They churned through song after song, and Jennifer and Jeff danced and screamed their lungs out. Flash even walked over to them and shook Jeff's hand.

After the encore, the lucky youngsters headed backstage and mingled with other guests as well as the band members. There were several people there, including members of local band Grey Wolf, who had opened the show.

Jeff saw other musicians as well, including Steve Conway from The Fifty-Eights, who remembered him from the school dance. It was a great atmosphere and an evening Jeff would never forget. T.J presented him with an autographed photo, which read:

Jeff, thanks for your help and stick with your writing, T.J.

As they walked to the taxi rank, Jeff lifted a Flame poster from the wall as a souvenir. Travelling home in the taxi, he asked Jennifer how T.J knew he wrote poetry?

'I read *Midnight Clouds* to him - and he loved it!' she said smiling. He looked at the signed photo once more and held her close to him. Once home, he burst through the front door and told his mum all about the evening and finally disclosed his secret to her.

'Oh, he looks quite wicked.' she commented, looking closely at Jeff's photograph.

'It's just his stage image. Anyway, I am beat,' said Jeff yawning, 'I'll see you in the morning Mum.'

'Yes, sleep well.' she said. Jeff was still smiling when he turned off the light. T. J's words of encouragement buzzed around his brain and he felt confident in furthering his writing skills. After all, T.J wrote songs which were loved by millions of people all over the world.

The next day Jeff slept in and then caught up on some Science and English homework. Cool winds and drizzling rain made it a perfect day to spend indoors. Bill called around late in the day, wanting confirmation that it was Jeff who Flash had acknowledged from the stage last night.

'Awesome!' said his friend in disbelief. He nearly fainted when Jeff produced the autographed photo. They chatted until dinner time and Mrs Walker invited Bill to join them, which he did. She enjoyed seeing Bill again. When the boys were younger, Bill spent lots of his spare time in the Walker household.

'What are your plans for next year?' she asked him, hoping to sway Jeff's decision a little.

'I'm continuing on at school.' Bill answered. 'If I don't graduate, my folks would kill me!'

'Jeff's thinking of leaving school.' she said. Bill sat silently nodding his head.

'I think I'm making the right decision.' said Jeff in an assuring tone.

The next day at school signalled the start of 'Career Planning week', and while most students were dreading their interviews with the school's councillor, Jeff couldn't wait to get his plans for next year underway. As the students slowly made their way to class from assembly, Jeff and several others from his grade all jostled for a look at the notice board displaying their interview times.

'When is your interview?' asked Jan, sliding a stool up next to Jeff at their Science desk.

'After lunch.' he replied.

'Mine's at 11:30.' she said, pulling a tartan pencil case out of her bag.

'Do you have any idea what you'd like to do for a career?' he asked.

'No, not really.' she replied. 'But I know I'm interested in Forensic Science, so I might follow that path and see what happens.'

'Ugh' he blurted, pulling a face. 'Doesn't that mean doing tests on dead people?'

'Sometimes.' replied Jan grinning.

The morning passed rapidly, and Jeff was something of a minor celebrity, after word spread of his brush with rock 'n' roll fame. He met Jennifer and Tracey outside the gym for lunch.

'I really can't believe it all happened.' said Jennifer, still in a state of shock. 'It's almost like a dream y'know? Jeff are you listening?' she asked, after he failed to respond.

'Yeah, what?' he said.

'I was talking to you!' she snapped.

'Err sorry, I was miles away.' he replied.

'Are you OK?' asked Tracey, 'You don't seem yourself to-day.'

'I'm fine, just recovering from a big weekend that's all.' Jeff answered.

But his mind was pre-occupied with other things. Mostly, it was the fast-approaching interview with the school councillor, Mrs McGill. As the two girls chatted, he quietly ate his sandwich. The bell rang, signalling the end of lunch.

'I'll see you on the bus, OK?' said Jen.

'I think I might walk home. I'd like to be alone for a bit.' he said, getting to his feet.

'Fine!' said Jennifer, throwing her bag over her shoulder. She stormed off with Tracey in tow.

'What's with him today?' quizzed Tracey.

'Oh, he's just got things on his mind, that's all' answered Jennifer. 'I am a little confused though, as we had such a great time at the Flame concert.' The two girls stopped walking.

'You don't suppose he's.... nah.' blurted Tracey, stopping mid-sentence.

'He's what?' demanded Jennifer. Her friend looked away before replying.

'Met someone else?' finished Tracey.

'No way.' said Jennifer, shaking her head. 'Jeff's not like that.'

The two girls looked at each other before walking on.

'You're probably right,' said Tracey, 'it's just that he wasn't his usual self today, and you may not have noticed, but there's been another couple of occasions where he's been really quiet during lunch time as well, just like today.'

Jennifer looked at her friend and shook her head again.

'He loves me and is obviously worried about the next twelve months is all. Nothing more than that.' said Jen

As the two girls made their way to their next lesson, Jeff was sitting in the school library with his English class. His classmates were particularly rowdy, and Mr Daubney was on the receiving end of various projectiles.

'That's it. I've had enough. Everyone can stay late and help to file returned books.' roared the librarian. Jeff noted the time and made his way to the arranged interview with the councillor.

'Sit down Walker!' demanded Daubney. But Jeff kept walking, in a world of his own and oblivious to the classroom chaos of his peers. A few unruly kids would not dampen his enthusiasm. *They may not take careers week seriously, but I am,* he thought aloud.

He knocked on room 24B.

'Hello Jeff, please come in.' said Mrs McGill. Although she had been employed at the school for some time, this was the first occasion Jeff had met with her. Jeff guessed she was in her late thirties and judging by the novels that were scattered around her office, loved reading. She had a pleasant demeanour and Jeff liked her immediately. He'd gone in with an open mind and was ready to listen to any advice she had to offer.

'Let's get started, shall we?' she said with a friendly smile.

'Well, I'm not completely sure what I want to do.' he began, 'but I like creative writing and poetry as well. Finding work as an author, or just writing, is something that I believe could make me happy.' said Jeff. 'I've got some of my work to show you.' he added and produced various poems from his bag. After carefully reading over each poem, Mrs McGill smiled and then spoke.

'They're beautiful Jeff. These poems evoke some strong emotions.'

He smiled awkwardly. The conversation continued for a further twenty minutes before concluding.

'It's been lovely to meet you, Jeff. I'll make some enquiries over the next few days on your behalf, OK?' she said.

'That sounds great.' replied Jeff, delighted with her response.

'Just one more thing.' asked the councillor, as he was opening the door.

'Can I keep a copy of *Midnight Clouds* for myself? That one, is wonderful.'

Jeff felt warm inside, pleased that his words had made another person feel good.

'Well, of course you can.' he replied.

He was filled with elation and after exiting Mrs McGill's office, jumped in the air and breathed a sigh of relief.

Before too long, the final bell for the day had rung. Jeff felt buoyant as he strode along the sidewalk for home.

What a great day, he thought, whilst kicking an empty cola can for part of the journey.

'Hi Mum.' he yelled.

'I'm in the backyard.' his mother replied. He explained to her how positive the meeting with the councillor had been, and how much she had liked his poems.

'She even wanted a copy for herself!' he exclaimed.

'Well done Jeff, I'm immensely proud of you.'

Getting up off her knees, Mrs Walker collected the pile of weeds she had pulled from the garden and placed them into a bucket.

'Would you mind visiting the grocery store to buy a few things?' she asked.

'I'd love to.' said Jeff cheerfully.

'It's good to see you so happy.' said his mum. Jeff raced over to where she was standing, clasped her hands and led her in an impromptu dance.

'I feel great!' he shouted, adding 'I just know things will work out.'

She smiled and gave him that concerned look that only a mother can give.

'I hope they do.' she replied.

He jumped on his skateboard and returned from the store an hour later with an armful of groceries.

'What took you so long?' asked his mother.

'I lost track of time playing pinball.' he replied. She frowned.

After a filling dinner of roast chicken and vegetables, Jeff washed and dried the dishes, then joined his mother in the living room.

'All finished.' he said

'Thanks Jeff, you're a big help. Can I ask you for another favour?' she asked. Jeff nodded. 'Would you mind having a look at the vacuum cleaner, it was making weird noises this afternoon, as if something's clogged.'

He located the cleaner, then lugged it out the back door and into the garage.

The time was around a quarter to eight when there was a knock at the front door.

I wonder who that could be at this hour? thought Mrs Walker.

She opened the door and was greeted by Jennifer's smiling face.

'Hi Mrs Walker, is Jeff home?' she asked politely.

'Yes, he is, please come through.' she answered. 'He's in the garage, and it's Barbara - not Mrs Walker.' Jennifer shrugged her shoulders and smiled awkwardly.

'Thanks, Barbara.' she replied softly.

Jennifer exited the house via the back door and walked towards the garage. She stood outside on the grass for a moment, silently observing Jeff as he worked on the appliance.

But this was by no means a social visit. Ever since Tracey had mentioned that silly idea that Jeff had met someone else, Jennifer could not get it out of her head. There was only one way to put her mind at ease and to restore her confidence in him.

'Hi there.' she blurted, startling him a little.

'Hello stranger, what a surprise.' he replied smiling. 'What are you doing here?'

'Oh, I was thinking about you all afternoon and I thought I'd surprise you.' said Jen, wrapping herself in his arms. She listened intently as Jeff showed her the inner workings of a vacuum cleaner, knowledge he had gained from watching his father at work. Then Jen casually mentioned what had been worrying her.

'You were miles away today, is everything alright?' she asked.

'Of course.' replied Jeff.

'I mean with us; everything's OK isn't it?' she added.

'What's on your mind?' he asked curiously. She looked away from him.

'You haven't met somebody else, have you?' Jennifer asked glumly.

Jeff broke into a smile and placed his outstretched hands on her shoulders.

'Wait right here.' he said, then disappeared inside the house. He returned a couple of minutes later clutching a piece of paper.

'Read this.' he said, handing her a copy of his most recent poem, *Sleeping Sea*.

He watched her eyes intently as they read over each verse. They soon welled with tears and she hugged him tightly.

'Listen to me,' said Jeff, 'you are the most important person in my life. I love you.' Jennifer sobbed happily in his arms. He wiped the tears from her cheeks, then softly kissed her damp skin.

'I'm sorry.' she whispered.

'My mind was elsewhere today.' said Jeff. 'I have been preoccupied with all this career planning stuff. I've also been tied up with my studies, my writing, work, and of course Flame.' he added with a chuckle. She nodded. 'Let's put this vacuum cleaner back together and start it up.' he said.

They headed inside and joined Jeff's Mum in the living room.

'Any luck Jeff?' she asked.

'All fixed.' he replied, before plugging it in and giving a noisy demonstration.

'He's just like his Dad,' Mrs Walker commented to Jennifer. 'That man could repair anything.'

Jeff made some coffee and they spent the next hour or

so playing board games, including Chinese Checkers, a long-time favourite of his mother's.

'That's it for me.' yawned Jeff, after losing three straight games to his mum.

'Yeah, I'd better be off too, it's quite late.' added Jen.

'Take care on your way home.' said Mrs Walker, as Jeff called her a taxi. The young couple kissed passionately on the front porch before parting for the evening.

'She's cute, isn't she?' said his mum when he re-entered the house.

'Don't I know it.' he replied with a smirk.

'Well, I'm off to bed,' he said, 'but before I do, I think I'll write a letter to Uncle Jack, maybe cheer him up with a poem or some words of positivity.'

'That will be nice, he'll like that.' commented Mum. The aspiring young writer sat up until 1:30 AM, deeply engrossed in his letter.

Not surprisingly, he slept through the alarm as it did its thing the next morning. He quickly showered, then dressed and flew out the front door. Kicking his skateboard along the road, he made a brief stop at a post box and mailed the letter to his Uncle.

Jeff found most of the school day uninteresting.

A tedious, tiresome Tuesday, he thought to himself. 'I'll call it a triple T.' he mused. However, Mrs McGill's words of encouragement from the previous day had given him enough motivation to get through the boring classes.

| 13 |

Good Morning Mr Sunlight

He felt relieved to exit the school gates at 3.00 PM and make his way to the bus terminal. Once in the city, he descended from the bus. As he walked to the hotel, the honk from a passing car startled him. He turned to see police officers Turner and Lowe drive past him in their squad car. He waved to them and called out and was still chuckling to himself as he entered the foyer.

He saw Sandy chatting to a waitress from the restaurant. She looked attractive he thought, in a short black skirt and white blouse with frilly cuffs. Then he had a fast and anxious flashback to last Friday evening.

'Oh my god, I remember Sandy gave me a lift, but what else happened? I can't think, did I say anything or do anything?' These questions flickered through his mind. He smiled at her as he passed through the foyer, hoping she would remain locked in conversation.

'Hey, Jeff.' she blurted. 'Can we talk later?' He swung around and faced her.

'Sure.' he answered, before hurrying to the changing area.

He tried to cast his mind back to that evening, and if anything happened.

'I must've been drunker than I thought.' he mused. 'How many beers did Colt and Flash give me? I also recall drinking champagne, then sharing a bottle of whiskey with Flash. No wonder I was blitzed.'

He decided that avoiding Sandy for the evening would give him a chance to think back and recall the events of last Friday. He managed to avoid his admirer for most of the shift until she surprised him in the staff room.

'Where have you been?' asked Sandy, with her hands on her hips. 'I've been looking all over for you.'

'Well, you've found me.' uttered Jeff.

'Let's sit down shall we.' she said, pulling a chair out from the table. There were a few moments of silence as Sandy stared directly at Jeff and seemed to be choosing her words carefully. It was too much for him to bear.

'Listen if I said or did anything, I apologize.' he blurted. 'I honestly can't remember.' Sandy looked at him strangely.

'What are you talking about?' she asked.

'Last Friday night, I remember you driving me home.'

'Oh, that,' giggled Sandy, 'I've forgotten all about that.'

'Did I do anything stupid?' he asked. Sandy wanted to remind him of what he had said to her and of their kiss but decided to keep those moments to herself.

'You were just a little loud was all.' she replied.

'Phew.' exclaimed Jeff, relieved.

'Now, is it alright if I continue?' she asked.

'Go ahead.'

'I think I have mentioned to you about the art class I've

been attending. They are a great group of people who are all very creative. Anyway, they're holding a dinner this Saturday night and I would like you to accompany me.'

Jeff sat pondering for a few seconds, thinking of what he could be getting himself into. Was this wise? Yet he remembered her being alone at the movies and, feeling sympathetic, wanted to help her. He nodded and smiled.

'I'd love to.' he replied.

'Great. It will be a fun night.' said Sandy, before getting a coffee from the machine and strutting back to her desk. Jeff swallowed the last few mouthfuls of his cola, then got back to work. He was pleased that Sandy had asked him and was more than happy to help her out - as a friend. However, one question remained lodged in his brain; should he tell Jennifer? He pondered it repeatedly.

'I'm just helping out a friend that's all, Jen won't mind.' he assured himself.

On his way home, he stopped by a phone booth at the bus station. He wanted to quickly call Jen and tell her about the dinner with Sandy, but couldn't go through with it.

'I'll tell her at school tomorrow.' he said aloud. As he was about to board the bus to Key Valley, he heard someone calling his name. He turned to see Rick, poking his head out the window from a stationary bus.

'How ya' doin' Jeff?'

'I'm doing great. Quite busy actually.' replied Walker.

'You need to relax more, wind down a little,' said Rick. 'I hear you and Flame are good buddies.' he added with a laugh. Jeff nodded his head and smiled. 'Listen, why don't you come around to my place this Friday night, I'm having a few friends over.' asked Rick.

'Right On. I'll be there.' replied Jeff, as Rick's bus began to pull away.

'It's 156 Raleigh Road, Harlington or just ask Susan if you forget.' yelled Rick loudly. Jeff gave him the 'thumbs-up' and then boarded his bus for Key Valley. After an evening of TV with his mum, he slept soundly, then left for school early the next day.

Not too many more days here, he thought, as he entered the school grounds.

Jennifer ran up to greet him enthusiastically, and he decided that this was as good a time as any to sound her out about his upcoming dinner.

'You're here early Mr Walker.' she said, giving him a peck on the cheek.

'I know, I skipped doing homework last night and I've got to catch up.' he replied.

'Come and sit with me for a while.' she begged, 'before the bell goes, pleeaasse. I won't see you all day.' whined Jennifer.

'Now how can I refuse such a pretty face?' he answered, running the back of his hand over her soft skin. The young couple sat down by a tree, and Jeff listened intently as his girlfriend told him all about the mischief that her younger brother was getting himself into at home.

'Sounds as though young Randy's bored.' he commented.

'I know,' said Jen, 'he's been asking *when is Jeff coming over to play with me* again?' Jeff scratched his head.

'Hey, you could come over on Saturday, and maybe even stay for dinner!' blurted Jennifer excitedly.

'I actually want to talk to you about Saturday night.' said Jeff.

'Go on.' she said, clutching his arm tightly.

'Well, the thing is, Sandy, the lady from work who I've told you about....' he said, as the smile on Jennifer's face began to fade.

'You've mentioned her before but continue.' said Jennifer.

'She's asked me to accompany her to dinner or something for her art school. I told her I would, and I just thought I should let you know about it, that's all.' he finished.

Jennifer turned her head to one side then ran her fingers through her hair. A few silent seconds ticked by before she spoke.

She's just a friend, isn't she Jeff?' she asked firmly.

He sighed. 'How can you ask me that, after what I told you on Monday night?'

Jennifer looked up the fast-moving clouds.

'I just had to ask.' she said.

He put his hand on her knee.

'Yes, we're just friends. She's a nice person, but quite lonely.'

Feeling a little guilty after expressing her jealousy, Jennifer whispered 'Sorry' in his ear before cuddling him tightly. The bell rang out, signalling the call for assembly.

'See ya.' said Jeff,

'Are we meeting for lunch?' asked Jen

'Not today, I've got to get that homework done.' he replied.

First class of the day was Geography, and the teacher, Mr Hibbs was in a strange mood, or so Jeff thought.

'Erin, please name me the capital of France?' asked Hibbs.

'Paris.' answered the girl in front of Jeff. Mr Hibbs was a short man, with thick black hair, which was always immaculately styled. His eyes scanned over the students as if searching for a sucker.

'Mr Pender, name me food from France please.' he asked. Pender looked worried as he searched for an answer.

'Monsieur Hibbs, I like zee french fries.' he replied, in a woeful French accent. 'No wait, zay are not from France, zay are cooked in Greece!' he joked.

Mr Hibbs turned a bright red and all of the class, except for Jeff, erupted into laughter.

'Actually Pender, the origin of the French Fry is disputed by both Belgium and France. Other culinary delights, such as escargot or the baguette would have been more acceptable answers. I have no time for clowns Pender, especially ones who would be lucky to point out Europe on a globe. Since you do such a wonderful French impersonation, maybe you should go and show it to Mr Green!' said Hibbs, pointing towards the Principal's office.

Pender reluctantly threw his books in his school bag, then exited the room. That was the only real highlight from an otherwise slow and uninteresting class. The students were also given a small assignment to do.

I'll get that done at lunch as well, thought Jeff, trudging to his next class.

12:30 rolled around and Jeff spent over an hour, all of his

lunch time, completing his overdue homework. At the completion of the school day, he met Jen at the bus line up.

'Hey.' he said walking up behind her.

'Did you get all your work done?' she asked.

'Sure did, which means I can spend all afternoon and this evening immersed in creative writing.'

They spent the ride home chatting and laughing. Jeff said goodbye and jumped off the bus. When he walked in the house, he was greeted by his mum's smiling face.

'You're happy, what's up?' he questioned curiously.

'There's a surprise for you on your bed.' she said grinning.

Jeff rushed to his bedroom and eagerly ripped open the large package. He could not believe his eyes when he saw it. It was a brand-new typewriter. He opened the box and held it up.

'What's this for?' he asked excitedly.

'All good writers must have the best equipment.' she replied.' Jeff was ecstatic.

'I can't believe it.' he shrieked, 'I've been thinking about getting one for ages!'

He hugged his mother.

'I'd better get dinner started.' she said, leaving his bedroom.

Jeff could not wait to try out his new 'toy,' so he quickly changed and then settled in behind his typewriter. He stared at it, as it sat gleaming on his desk. A brand-new, Brother Deluxe 700T that even came with a carry case.

'Made in Nagoya, Japan.' he said aloud, reading the sticker on the machine. *I'd like to travel there someday,* he thought.

He spent the next couple of hours, searching his mind for the right words to piece together. His Mum brought dinner into his room and smiled proudly as he worked.

Late in the evening, he rubbed his eyes and pulled the paper from the typewriter. Feeling satisfied, he sat back on his bed to inspect his work. Jeff read aloud what he had written:

Good morning Mr Sunlight how are you today ?
I love the way you warm my face and chase my dreams away
Good morning Mrs Blackbird please don't fly away
Your morning call has given me a smile
that I'll carry around all day
Good morning Mr Raindrop how long will you stay ?
I hope it's long enough to wash my failures all away
Good evening Mr Rainbow, the rain has made me cold
So may I climb up to the sky and find my pot of gold ?
Good evening Mrs Sunset you feel so warm and kind
I close my eyes and think of my bad memories left behind
Goodnight now Mr Moonlight the stars are close to you
Your glowing smile covers my face
and I'll dream the whole night through

Having read over the poem one final time, he decided to title it *'Good Morning Mr Sunlight.'* He yawned then switched off the light and quickly fell asleep. It would be the first of many poems created on that typewriter.

Thursday got off to another hectic start, but the day turned out to be an enjoyable one. Jeff headed to work and arrived just as Sandy was leaving for the day.

'Not working tonight?' he asked.

'No, I've got an art class, by the way I'll pick you up at about seven-ish on Saturday.' she said, before pulling out onto the street in her beetle.

He passed Alan Cusack in the foyer.

'Can you see me before you leave tonight?' said his boss.

'Yes sir.' replied Walker. 'I wonder what he wants.' he mused.

Good evening Max.' he said, approaching his colleague.

'Jeff, what's happening?'

'Not a lot, how are things around here today.'

'Kind of slow, but there's a basketball team checking in some time tonight, so I'm glad it's you and not me.' said Max laughing. 'Listen, I hear you and Miss French have got a date lined up for Saturday.' added his curious friend.

'Do you do anything else with your time except gossip?' Jeff asked, shaking his head in disbelief.

'Well, what about it?'

'Keep your ears open Max, I'm sure you'll hear it through the grapevine.' said Jeff, leaving his colleague dying with curiosity.

Max was correct about it being a busy night, and Jeff was tired after accommodating not one, but two junior basketball teams. After he signed off, he knocked on Cusack's door as requested.

'Jeff, please come in.' said Alan Cusack. 'Sit down' he added, motioning towards a chair.

'Flame's management team were quite pleased with your service. Congratulations.' began his boss. 'You've been working quite hard lately haven't you?' he asked.

Jeff nodded. 'I do try sir.'

'Thankyou again for your help in getting Sandy back, we couldn't afford to lose someone with her experience.'

'That's OK,' said Jeff, 'we had a small misunderstanding, that's all.'

'Well, I'm glad it's all settled then.' commented Cusack. 'How would you like to work as Miss French's assistant?' he asked.

Jeff was taken aback. Yes, he had been working particularly hard, but an offer of promotion was unexpected. He had no hesitation in accepting.

'I'd really like that sir, thank you.' he replied.

'Good to hear. You will still be on the same hours, but you'll be taking orders from Sandy.' Jeff nodded then exited the office. As he walked out of the hotel, it was raining quite heavily. He stood under the awning of a donut store until the rain had eased.

Once home, he shared news of the job offer with his mum.

'That's great news Jeff. Hard work often reaps rewards.' she said.

Although excited at the promotion and the opportunity to engage in more interesting work, he was uncertain of how he and Sandy would work together. He hoped it would be cohesive. She had, after all, nearly resigned over this very situation.

Time will tell, I guess, he thought, scratching his head. Sitting at his desk, he re-read *Good Morning Mr Sunlight.* Feeling quite pleased with the finished product, he slipped the paper in a folder, along with his other poems.

Friday hurried by, with the only highlight being, that it signalled the end of the week. Jeff liked Fridays and the mood in the schoolyard was always noticeably different. This was of course due to the anticipation of the fast-approaching weekend!

Jeff had a couple of exciting days planned and was actually looking forward to Sandy's dinner.

'Want to come over to my house this evening?' Jen asked on the afternoon bus.

'I'd love to, but Rick invited me over to his place for a party. It's guys only, sorry.'

'Oh, well that's OK,' she replied, 'maybe we might do something on Sunday?'

Jeff nodded his head.

'What have you got lined up for the weekend?' he asked.

'Tracey and I are going clothes shopping tomorrow, and we'll head over to Susan's later in the day.'

'How could you need new clothes after your birthday?' questioned Jeff with a smirk.

'You can go shopping just to look y'know, but I usually never do.' she replied giggling.

'Just when is your birthday again Mr Walker?'

'A few weeks away, 29th November.' he answered.

'Seventeen, at last, huh!' she replied. Jeff pulled an amusing face before playfully pinching her cheek. 'You're a Sagittarius.' she said.

'That's right,' he acknowledged. 'My Mum once told me that my birthday falls on the 333rd day of the year. Apparently, people with the number 3 in their life are creative and have a strong personality - if you believe in that kind of stuff.'

Once home, Jeff collapsed in front of the television until dinner was ready.

'I told you I'm going over to Rick's tonight, didn't I?' he said to his mum.

'Yes you did, he's the boy with the motorbike, isn't he?'

'That's him.'

'Make sure you're home at a reasonable hour OK?' said his Mum.

'OK.' he answered.

After a shower, he put on some jeans and a shirt, then phoned for a taxi.

'Not another cab, Jeff,' said his mum from the sofa. 'You'll have to think about obtaining your driver's licence soon.'

'Great idea.' replied Jeff.

'Where does Rick live?' asked his Mum.

'Harlington.'

'That's a long way from here, let me get you some money.' said his Mum, reaching for her purse.

'No thanks Mum, you keep your cash.' said Jeff, refusing to accept his mother's kind gesture. A few minutes later, a car beeped and pulled into their driveway. Jeff hastily left the house.

'See you later Mum.' he blurted, before quickly poking his head back in the living room. 'You're the best, you know that, and I do love you.' he said, then slammed the front door shut.

| 14 |

The art class dinner

Fortunately, there was not much traffic on the road, and the taxi made good time getting over to Harlington, or 'Harlo' as the locals called it. Jeff walked the remaining fifty metres or so up Raleigh road, and eventually came to number 156. A tiny, single-story brick house, with a well-kept garden. The driveway was splattered with dark oil stains, a sure sign of motorcycle enthusiasts, and most definitely Rick's house!

He tapped loudly on the door and was greeted by his bike-riding buddy.

'Jeff, good to see you again, come on in.'

Three other boys were sitting in the living room, two watching TV, and the other reading a dirt bike magazine.

'Hey fellas, I'd like you to meet Jeff, Jeff this is Marty, Chet and Frank.' said Rick, pointing to his friends.

All five boys had a love of music and dirt biking, so they hit it off and enjoyed each other's company. Rick had already told the others of Jeff's incredible weekend with Flame, and he found himself cornered by his new friends, keen to hear more about it.

'Were they wearing makeup?', 'What's Colt like?', 'How was Marc? and 'Did you hold Flash's guitar.' were some of the many questions fired at Jeff soon after his arrival.

'Guys, ease up on the boy, he's here to relax.' piped Rick, 'let's order some beer and pizza!' he blurted, before raising the volume on the stereo.

'Where's your Dad?' asked Frank, a little concerned.

'He's gone with my Mum to some convention out of town. They'll be back tomorrow.' replied Rick, dancing around the room. He then put on his deepest voice, stood close to the stereo, and phoned through the order to the liquor store. He hung up the phone and then explained to the others what to do. 'Listen, they'll be here soon, so get in the bathroom and let the shower run.' he said, pointing to Chet. 'Jeff, you go with Frank and Marty and hang out in my bedroom. But keep the noise down.' he added.

Soon after ordering pizza, there was a knock at the door.

'Hi, is this number 156?' asked the delivery man.

'Sure is.' answered Rick, lowering the volume on the stereo. 'I'll just get my Dad.' he said, before walking away and calling out to his father. 'Hang on a minute.' shouted Rick, in the direction of the front door. 'He's in the shower, but I'll get some money off him.'

He returned a couple of minutes later with a slightly damp ten-dollar bill, which he handed over.

'Maybe I'd better wait until I see your Dad.' said the driver suspiciously.

'He's gonna be quite a while, he just got in, but he said you can keep the change.' said Rick.

The beer was handed over.

'Have a good night.' said the delivery man walking away.

'Don't worry we will!' uttered Rick as he slammed the door shut. The other boys quickly appeared and congratulated Rick on his acting prowess.

They each ripped open a can of Ashton Ale and Frank proposed a toast to Evel Knievel, the motorcycle stuntman who they all admired.

'I'd also like to welcome Jeff to tonight's 'A.A meeting.' laughed Chet, referencing the initials of the local brewing company whilst holding up a can.

'Man, that plan went like clockwork.' boasted Rick.

'Always does.' added Marty, as the pizza van pulled up.

By 12:30 AM, most of the beer had been consumed, and Frank and Chet lay sprawled out on the sofa. Rick was in the garage showing Jeff and Marty some new bike parts when he suddenly had the idea that they should all go for a late-night ride!

Jeff was so drunk he could barely walk and was in no condition to successfully manoeuvre a motorcycle. He watched Rick slowly ride around the backyard until he felt he would throw up, which he did.

'Way to go Walker!' yelled Rick, over the roar of his engine.

Jeff watched them ride out onto the road and stood there laughing as they rode away. The music was still blaring inside yet did not disturb Frank and Chet who were out to the world. Jeff thought he saw a patrol car quietly roll down the street and ran to the driveway to investigate.

The car swung around and drove towards him, but he quickly darted around the back of the house and hid behind the garage. Two officers got out from the vehicle with flash-lights and hollered at the front door.

'Police, please open the door.' said the female officer. They walked around the side of the house and peered in through an open window, noting the two boys crashed out on the sofa.

'Hey!' she yelled again, 'turn that music off.'

'They can't hear.' replied her partner. 'My guess is they're very drunk.' he added, pointing to the empty cans scattered around the living room.

Jeff stood motionless until he suddenly felt the urge to vomit again. He walked a few paces behind the garage, then drunkenly stepped on an old sheet of iron. The noise at-tracted the attention of the cops as Jeff stood frozen.

'Hey there's someone out here.' said the male officer, walk-ing towards the garage.

Jeff's head pounded and he felt both nauseous and edgy. In a moment of drunken panic, he decided to make a run for it and flee!

He jumped the fence and landed awkwardly in the neigh-bour's compost heap. He got to his feet and ran quickly, scal-ing their fence and into another backyard. There were several wrecked cars, some of which had been invaded by long grass and weeds. He stood against the fence trying to catch his breath when a light from the house flicked on and a black Doberman came hurtling from the back door – straight for him!

'What the hell?!' shrieked Jeff, as he dashed across the yard and up over another fence, as the snarling dog snapped at his legs. He ran quickly down a walkway which led onto a foot-ball field. He sat down on the oval in the darkness and regained his breath. He had no idea why he ran from Rick's place and even less of an idea of where he was.

Getting to his feet, he decided to head in the direction of a shopping mall that he could see in the distance. He stumbled drunkenly along the side of the road, cussing dogs and singing Flame songs as he went. Noticing a taxi coming towards him, Jeff ran out to the middle of the road and waved his arm.

'Hey stop.' he pleaded. The cab slowed down to pick him up.

'Where to son?' asked the driver.

'Key, key, key valley.' Jeff answered drunkenly.

As soon as he put his head back in the seat, he fell asleep, only to be awoken by the driver asking for a street name. He was never so happy to see his house and opened the car door before the vehicle had stopped.

'Hey buddy, you gonna pay me or what?!' demanded the driver.

Jeff pulled some cash from his wallet and slapped it in the driver's hand.

'Keep the change.' he mumbled, then staggered across the street to the front door.

The living room light was still on and the front door opened as he approached.

'Mum! You, you didn't have to wait up for me.' he slurred, stumbling into the house.

'What have you been up to? My gosh, just look at your clothes!' said his mother.

Jeff looked at his torn and muddy jeans and searched for the missing button from his shirt front.

'Damnit Jeff I've been worried about you.' Jeff gave a slight smirk before replying.

'Sorry Mum, I really need the toilet.'

He ran to the bathroom and threw up once again.

His mum helped him out of his dirty clothes then made him take a shower.

'We'll talk about this tomorrow.' she said and closed his bedroom door.

But Jeff was fast asleep.

Mrs Walker was angry with her son and determined to teach him a lesson. At around half-past seven the next morning, she decided to vacuum the house, in particular - the room adjacent Jeff's. It did the trick as he surfaced soon after holding his forehead.

'What time is it?' he groaned.

'Seven-thirty.' chirped his mother.

He collapsed into a chair in the kitchen and shut his eyes.

'What would you like for breakfast dear?' questioned his Mum. 'Some pork sausages or bacon and eggs?'

He winced.

'Ugh, no food.' he replied, pulling a long face.

'It won't take me long to fry up some hash browns. How many could you stomach, six or seven?' she added, smiling.

'Stop it, Mum, please.' he protested. 'I'll just get a glass of water.'

His Mum began chomping into a bowl of cereal and studied him carefully.

'So, you want to tell me about last night?'

'There's not much to tell.' he replied gingerly. 'I went over to Rick's and came home.'

She waited.

'That's it?!' she said. 'Come on, you can do better than that. Tell me the truth please Jeffery.'

He slowly recountered the previous evening's activities and she listened on curiously.

'Why would you run when seeing the police?'

'I don't know, I wasn't thinking. It was a stupid thing to do.' he replied.

'You're right about that. Jeff, tonight you will stay home and think about your behaviour. Maybe catch up on some study as well.' said his Mum.

'You are kidding, I hope!?' blurted Jeff.

She picked up her bowl and spoon from the table and took them to the sink.

'I am deadly serious.' she replied sternly.

'But I promised Sandy.' he cried.

'Well you'll have to unpromise her. I'm not changing my mind.' she confirmed, before storming off.

'Great.' he said under his breath.

Jeff felt seedy so went and took a long shower to help him wake up. It was another glorious Autumn day. He sat out in the backyard watching his mother work in her vegetable garden, wondering how a fantastic weekend could suddenly turn sour.

'Need any help?' he asked, trying to smooth her over a little.

'No thank you Jeffery Alan.' she replied. Usually when she called him that, she was angry with him. His mother would occasionally insert his Dad's name into the conversation to emphasise her disappointment with him. Jeff went to his room and returned with a note pad. Sitting down on the soft grass, he closed his eyes and wrote whatever entered his mind. Although he still felt the remains of a rotten hangover, the sun caressing his face helped him to feel better.

He let his vivid imagination run wild and wrote a poem which he titled, *A Carefree Autumn Day*

Sun streams down upon my back, beautiful cloudless skies
My face is warm and sound asleep, I gently close my eyes
Spiderweb dances with the breeze, a butterfly is at play
Sunlight breathes to caress my neck, a carefree Autumn day
Sunflowers caught in conversation, the hum of a busy bee
Pigeon squints and softly sleeps in the casuarina tree
Ferntree drops a silent tear, an aging tree branch groans
Moggy stretches and gently yawns, upon the cobblestones
A goldfish hides under lily pads, like an orange submarine
Pokes his head to suck some air
then floats back down the stream
Pinecones sit in groups of five and view the world below
A sparrow darts down from the trees to say a quick hello
A peewee squawks and sings for joy
then performs an amusing dance
she flicks her beak through blades of grass
and plucks out bugs and ants
Last night's moon has nearly died

at the start of a brand new day
I watch him drown in a blue-sky tide
as he frowns and fades away

'Jeff, your lunch is ready.' hollered his mother from the kitchen. He stood up and stretched.

'Didn't you hear me calling before?' she asked, as he entered the house.

'No, I had the head down.' he replied holding up his note pad.

'What did you write about?'

'Autumn. Here, take a look.' he added, handing her the pad. After reading it a couple of times, she broke into a smile.

'That's really nice Jeff. Who'd have thought that my son was a poet.' she said proudly.

Jeff sat hungrily devouring a chicken and lettuce sandwich, hoping his poem may have swayed his Mum's mind a little. But he decided to hold back a little longer before asking again. After lunch, Mum resumed her gardening and Jeff sat at the table adjusting his most recent poem when the phone rang.

'Hello.' he said, hoping it would be Jen.

'Hi, is that Jeff?' asked the female voice.

'Yes, it is. This sounds like Sandy. How are you?'

'Very excited about tonight. I forgot to tell you it's a black-tie dinner, so I'm just letting you know.' she said.

'Thankyou. I had better get my tux ready.'

'OK great, I will see you at seven. Bye.' she added.

How could I tell her? She's got her heart set on it, mused Jeff, listening to the disconnect tone. He decided it was now or never and trudged out to the garden to confront his mother again.

'Hey Mum, that was Sandy on the phone.' There was a long, silent pause. 'She's excited about tonight. Please, could you reconsider? I won't get into any trouble, I promise.' he begged.

His mother looked up from her gardening and gazed at him. Since becoming a single parent, she often found it hard to discipline him. When required, she did pull him into line, however the term 'strict parent' could not be applied to Barbara Walker. In fact, after Jeff's father had died, her affection for her son had grown and she doted on her only child.

'Alright,' she conceded, 'but no more getting into trouble OK?'

Jeff was elated and he ran over and kissed her. She took him up on his earlier offer of gardening help, and he spent part of the afternoon working up a sweat in the backyard.

'I'm heading inside to take a shower.' he said.

'It's time I stopped for the day anyway.' she replied, cleaning the dirt from her hands. 'You don't want any supper, is that right?' she asked.

'No thanks.' replied Jeff.

After his shower, he ran a razor over his face and splashed on some aftershave, still in its box from Christmas. He danced and sang, shuffling in front of the bathroom mirror. He sure as hell couldn't move like James Brown but that didn't matter. His spirit was high, and his mood was happy regardless.

Dead on seven o'clock, Sandy's shiny red v-dub pulled into the driveway.

'Jeff your lift is here.' hollered his Mum, surveying the attractive older woman from behind the living room curtain.

'Get away from there Mum, she'll see you.' snapped Jeff, on his way to answer the door.

'Hi there.' said Sandy.

'You look great.' replied Jeff. 'Come in and meet my mother.'

She stepped inside the house.

'Mum, I'd like you to meet Sandy French,' said Jeff politely.

'Lovely to meet you Mrs Walker.' offered Sandy with a handshake.

'Please, call me Barbara.' said Jeff's Mum. 'Can I get you anything?'

'No thank you, we must get going. It was nice meeting you Barbara.' she added with a smile.

'See you Mum.' said Jeff, following his friend out the door.

'Psst Jeff.' whispered his Mum.

'What?' said Jeff returning.

'She's a little old isn't she?' she said, pulling an odd face.

'Good night Mum.'

'Is that aftershave I can smell?' asked Sandy when they sat in the car.

'It is.'

'It smells quite sexy.' she added, pressing her nose against his cheek.

'We'd better go.' he blurted, cranking the volume on her car stereo. 'So, where's this event located?'

'At a restaurant over in Winvale.' replied Sandy. She put her foot on the gas and increased the volume on the stereo even more. People on the sidewalk turned their heads, as Aerosmith played loudly from the beetle's speakers.

'Hey, I hear we're going to be seeing a lot of each other at work from now on.' she shouted, over the music.

'You know about that?' he asked surprised.

'Of course!' she replied.

'Alan asked me how I felt about it and I said it's cool.'

She stared at him for a moment then returned her eyes to the road. Jeff felt relaxed as he watched the scenery pass by from the car window.

'What time did Mummy say you had to be home?' she asked, teasing him.

'Whenever.' replied Jeff, trying to sound a little older than he was. The mood between the couple was friendly, and Sandy's obvious flirting didn't go unnoticed by Jeff.

They pulled into the restaurant's carpark and got out.

'We may as well look like we're a couple.' said Sandy, holding Jeff's hand. They found their table and were joined by other guests. Sandy's friend Yvette arrived late and sat opposite Jeff.

'Hello there.' she said to him.

'Hi.' he replied politely.

'Jeff, this is Yvette.' said Sandy, introducing him.

'He's cute.' Yvette whispered to her friend. It was obvious there was a little rivalry between the two girls.

'Where's your date tonight?' Sandy asked smiling, before taking a sip of white wine.

'Something came up.' answered Yvette.

'So, Jeff, Sandy tells me you're a writer.' she said, changing the conversation.

'Yeah I'm hoping to do something in that line of work when I leave school later this year.' he said.

'Really, how wonderful!' she giggled. 'You mean you're still at school? You look much older. I'd have said about twenty-one or twenty-two.' Yvette added.

'Can I get you a drink Jeff?' asked Sandy.

'No thanks, I'm still recovering from last night.'

'If you're going to the bar Sandra, I'll have a gin and tonic please.' asked Yvette with a smirk.

'You look lovely Yvette.' commented Jeff. She did. Dressed in a strapless black dress, with a stunning set of Akoya pearls, which nestled around her slender neck. She had green eyes and beautiful curly, auburn hair which sat on her shoulders.

'Why thank you, Jeff, you look quite handsome yourself.' Jeff felt her foot run up the inside of his leg.

'Here we are.' said Sandy, returning with the drinks. The evening rolled on, and Jeff was excited to see a wonderful display of artwork in the adjoining room.

'That's amazing.' he said, looking over Sandy's landscape. 'The colours are so vivid.'

'Thankyou cutie.' she replied, gulping on another wine. 'Come have a look at mine.' begged Yvette, dragging him by the arm.

'It's a portrait of my sister.' she exclaimed proudly.

'It's lovely.' he offered. After a three-course meal, it was time to hit the dance floor, but despite constant pleas from Yvette, Jeff remained at the table with Sandy, who was by this stage already quite drunk.

Although lodged behind the table, Yvette managed to grab Jeff and wrench him onto the dance floor, leaving Sandy to continue with her drinking. She downed the booze and giggled at the same time, pausing to stare at her friend dancing with the guy she loved.

Jeff returned to her after about twenty minutes, quite concerned with her alcohol intake.

'C'mon Sandy I think it's time we left.' She looked at him.

'You two look good on the dance floor.' she slurred jealously.

Unexpectedly, Yvette gave Jeff a farewell kiss on the lips. He quickly pulled away and politely said goodnight. He walked Sandy to the lounge area, propping her onto a sofa. Pulling out a coin, he called his mum and told her of the situation.

'Mum it's me, Jeff, sorry to wake you. Listen, Sandy's had too much to drink, so we're gonna catch a cab and I may even crash on her sofa or something.'

'You are making me worry, don't you get into any trouble young man.'

'I won't. Goodnight.'

It's nearly morning!' she blurted back.

Jeff glanced at his watch and noticed it was 2:15 AM.

'Where are we going?' asked Sandy, hanging onto Jeff, and staggering down the staircase to the street.

'We're jumping in a cab and dropping you off home.'

'What?' she blurted. 'I'm not leaving my car here! It'll get ripped off in this area.'

She's got a point, he thought. He looked in his wallet and realised he had spent most of his cash getting home from Rick's the previous evening.

'How much money you got on you?' he asked.

'About two dollars.' she giggled.

'Great, we haven't even got enough for cab fare.' he mused.

'No problem,' she said, 'I'll drive.'

'Problem,' replied Jeff, 'you can barely stand.'

Sandy stared at him for a moment, blinking her eyes.

'You drive, it's not that far.' she said, tossing him the keys. Jeff stood staring at the set of keys, glistening under the street light. Driving was no problem as his Dad had taught him the basic skills over many long trips together. The issue was, obviously, that he did not possess a driver's licence.

He remembered what his mother had said about not getting into trouble and sighed.

'We could walk.' offered Sandy, swaying along the sidewalk.

'Get in.' said Jeff, throwing caution to the wind.

'Go the back streets, I'll show you.' said Sandy.

'No, we'll just go the normal route and act as inconspicuous as possible.' he replied.

'I'm beat.' said Sandy, reclining the front seat. Jeff started the car and slowly drove off in the direction of Sandy's apartment, no more than a fifteen-minute drive.

'Which way now?' he asked, coming to an intersection. 'Sandy?' he asked again. But she was fast asleep.

'Guess I'll go it alone then.' he muttered, trying to recall the route she had taken a few hours earlier.

Jeff performed well for someone who had never driven on a sealed road before. His inexperience, however, saw him round a corner too fast and pass through a stop sign. A patrol car, passing in the opposite direction swung around and increased its speed.

Great, he thought, *I'm a goner.* But much to his relief, the police car increased its speed and flew right by him, in pursuit of another car! He looked skyward and said, 'I owe you one.'

After a couple of wrong turns, he eventually pulled the beetle to a stop outside Sandy's apartment.

'Sandy we're home, wake up.' he whispered, but she was out of it. Only one thing to do. Jeff lifted her out of the vehicle, then carried her up the stairs and into her apartment.

'Here we are.' he said, placing her gently on her double bed.

'Turn right here.' she said, opening one eye then laughing.

'You're home now Sandy. Get some sleep. I need to head back to Key Valley.'

'Hey, Walker.' she said. He turned. 'It drove me crazy to see you with Yvette tonight, I couldn't bear it. That's why I drank so much. I love you and can't live without you, please give me a chance.' she blurted hysterically.

'Sandy, you're drunk.' said Jeff.

'I know what I'm saying, I need you.' she yelled.

'Shh, you'll wake everyone.'

'I don't care!' she said, then closed her eyes and softly started to cry. Jeff walked over to her.

'Don't cry.' he said softly, moving her hair from her eyes. 'Hop into bed.' he added, pulling back her sheets. She stripped down to her underwear and clambered in. He hugged her, then kissed her on the forehead. 'Goodnight.' he whispered. As he moved away, she yanked him close to her and gave a quick, forceful kiss. He gently pulled away and smiled at her. Sandy mumbled something then closed her weary eyes and nodded off.

Exhausted, Jeff walked into the small living room, took off his dinner jacket and sat down on the sofa.

What an evening, he thought. He glanced at the clock which read 3:06 AM. He undid his tie then lay back to rest, propping a cushion under his head. He dragged his jacket over him and then he too fell asleep.

He awoke just after nine to find a soft pillow under his head and a thick blanket covering him. He yawned and rubbed his eyes. After folding the blanket, he checked on Sandy who was sound asleep. He shut her bedroom door, then quietly crept out of the apartment and onto the street. He tucked his shirt in and walked wearily along the sidewalk. He kept his eye out for a cab whilst trying to thumb a lift. He wasn't keen on hitchhiking and only did that when desperate - a couple of local kids had vanished whilst hitchhiking some time back, and their disappearances had rocked the community. A taxi eventually stopped, and the driver accepted Jeff's word that he would pay the fare at his destination.

| 15 |

Jealous

'Did you have a nice evening?' asked his mum, looking up from a magazine.

'Don't ask.' he replied on his way to his room. 'I'll tell you all about it in a sec.' he added, rushing past her with cash for the taxi driver.

He flopped down next to her and thirstily sank a big glass of juice.

'Mum,' he sighed, 'I think I'm ready to get my driver's licence.'

After sharing his story, she sounded relieved that he was not hurt or injured. She looked at him for a moment - dismayed by his decision to drive unlicenced.

'I asked you not to get in any trouble, yet you drove a car without a licence! I understand your reasons for doing so but that's just asking for trouble – and lots of it.' She flicked through the pages of the magazine without looking at him then sighed. 'Jeff, you're just going to have to tell this woman that you love Jennifer, she'll understand I'm sure.'

He paused.

'Her name's Sandy mum and I sure hope you're right.'

Jeff yawned and went to straight to bed, hoping to catch up on some much-needed sleep. However, feelings of guilt flooded his head, preventing him from falling into a deep sleep.

He resurfaced around 2:30 in the afternoon and prepared some strong coffee. Try as he might, the events of last night were weighing on his conscience and he could not relax.

Although he was no expert in the field of love and relationships, he felt in his head, that he was in no way cheating on Jennifer. Yet his heart told him otherwise, which explained the uneasy feeling.

I like Sandy and value her friendship. That's not cheating, he thought. *Nevertheless, I think I might drop in and say hello to Jen. It would make me feel better.*

He picked up the phone and called her.

'Hi Mrs Moore, this is Jeff, is Jen there?' There was a long pause.

'Erm, I'm sorry Jeff, she's um, Jen's not here at the moment' she answered, sounding evasive.

'Well, what time are you expecting her home?'

'Soon.' she replied.

'I see, I'm thinking of swinging by this afternoon, can you let her know I'll be stopping in please?' he said.

Another pause.

'Um, OK, I will pass the message on.'

That's odd. Something's up, he thought and headed to the garage.

'I'm going over to see Jen.' he yelled, to his mum in the

garden. She smiled and waved. He secured his helmet, then kick-started his Honda.

When he arrived at the Moore residence, he could see Randy playing on the street with a couple of friends. They all raced up to greet him.

'Hi Jeff, can you take me for a ride?' pleaded Jen's little brother.

'Maybe another time.' he answered. 'Is your sister home?'

'Yeah, she's in her room.' replied Randy.

'Catch you guys later.' said Jeff, who wheeled his bike down the driveway.

'Hello there Jeff.' said Mrs Moore greeting him at the front door. 'It's not really a good time.' she whispered. Jeff gave her a bewildered look.

'Why? What's going on?' he asked.

'Jennifer's upset.' interrupted her father from the living room.

'Well, can I see her?' Jeff asked with a concerned voice.

'I don't know.' replied Mrs Moore.

Walker stood in the doorway feeling very confused. He watched Mrs Moore walk to the bottom of the staircase.

'Honey, Jeff's here to see you.' she hollered.

'I'm busy, tell him to come back some other time.' Jennifer shouted.

'What?!' uttered Jeff, 'This is crazy, I want to know what's going on here.' he said, stepping inside the house then ascending the stairs to her bedroom.

'Jen, what's wrong?' he asked upon entering. He could see her eyes were red from crying.

'What do you care?!' she snapped back, as he sat beside her on the bed.

'Please tell me why you're so upset?' he asked again.

'Did you have a nice time last night?' she sobbed. Distressed, he scratched his neck.

'It was alright, I suppose.' replied Jeff, wondering what that had to do with anything.

'Why?'

'Well, I'd say you had a wonderful night Jeff. Because my Dad saw you leaving your friend's apartment earlier this morning!'

'Is *that* what this is all about?' he said. 'Sandy and I are just friends! She got very drunk and I had to drive her home. It was extremely late, so I decided to stay over...on the sofa.'

'Spare me the details.' said Jennifer, now sobbing uncontrollably.

'Hey, don't cry.' he whispered, placing his hand on her shoulder.

'Don't touch me!' she yelled as tears streamed down her cheeks.

'But I haven't done anything.' he pleaded.

'Jeff, I think you'd better go.' said Mr Moore firmly, entering the room.

Jeff brushed past him and stormed out of the house. He revved up his bike and roared out of the driveway, booking it down Lincoln Place. He was furious with Jen and let out a scream from under his helmet.

I should go and talk to Sandy, he thought, but quickly changed his mind knowing it could make matters worse. He stopped at a park and sat quietly for some time, needing to re-gain his composure. Many thoughts raced through his mind. After half an hour or so, he brushed the grass from his clothes then slowly rode home. He toyed with the idea of writing his feelings down but was not in the mood. Relieved to see the day come to an end, he settled into bed and then fell asleep.

It took him some time to get moving the following morn-ing. Besides it being a Monday, he was not keen for another tussle with Jennifer. Things had been blown way out of pro-portion, yet he decided that a positive frame of mind was what was needed.

After breakfast, he stood deep in thought at the bus stop, which was drenched in sunshine. The school bus arrived, he took a deep breath and climbed on enthusiastically. Jennifer was sitting with Susan and Tracey on the back seat, so he headed towards them.

'Hi.' he said. No reply. Her two friends put their heads down.

'How are you today Jen?' he asked, but she looked the other way. He was stunned.

'Well, thanks very much, *friends*.' he said, then about-faced and found another seat. He could hear the three of them gossiping but couldn't care less.

Jeff was upset and felt hurt. Found guilty without a fair trial! Once at school, he decided that the library was a good place to find solace.

'Hello, Jeffery.' said a cheerful voice behind him. It was Mrs McGill.

'Hi.' he said, warming to her friendly smile.

'I've got some great news for you.'

'I sure need some.' he replied.

'I contacted a few night schools and some colleges too. The response was positive, and a couple expressed interest in accepting you next year' she said.

'That's great!' he shrieked.

'But you've got to obtain certain grades this year to qualify.' she added.

'I've been putting in the effort, Mrs McGill. Hopefully, my grades will get me over the line.' he replied.

'Here are some brochures and information for you to read over.' she said. 'Let me know in a couple of weeks what you decide to do. It's not too long before you leave school.' He nodded and thanked her.

Apart from Mrs McGill's positive news, the day rolled by and ended the same way it had started. Jeff spotted Jennifer reading alone on the school bus and attempted to make peace once again.

'Jen, how was your day?' he asked, sitting next to her. She lifted her head from the novel and glared coldly at him. He was desperate to share his good news with her and could not take much more of this 'no talk' treatment. 'Jen, please.' he pleaded. She rested the book on her lap, then stared out the window. 'This is crazy!' he blurted. 'I've done nothing wrong, yet you're treating me like your worst enemy. Cast your mind back Jen to all we've done together in the last few weeks, I love you and would never hurt you' he paused for a few moments to calm down, then suddenly signalled the bus to stop. 'When you get home, read over the poems I have given you, then decide for yourself how much you mean to me. But I'm not putting up with this for too much longer.'

He felt relieved to exit the bus and then walked the rest of the way home. He stormed through the front door and into his bedroom, slamming the door shut behind him. His mother checked in on him, and although she listened to the whole messy saga, there was little she could do to help. After dinner, Jeff decided he would call Sandy at the hotel and then meet her for a chat at a city café. Just as she answered the phone there was a knock at the front door. He hung up the phone and half jogged to open it.

It was Jennifer.

'Ahm, hi Jeff, can I come in?' she whispered.

'Of course, you can.'

Jen sat down on his bed and took a couple of deep breaths.

'I think I owe you an apology. I may have jumped to the wrong conclusion and I refused to let you tell me the full story. So that's what I'd like you to do for me now, and we'll get this whole thing cleared up.'

Jeff went to the kitchen and fetched her a cola, then slowly explained the events of Saturday evening. He also told her of his Friday night adventure at Rick's place.

'You really got chased by a savage dog?' she asked, laughing. Jeff nodded then pulled her close to him, embracing her tightly.

'I love you.' he whispered.

'I'm sorry.' she said, resting her head on his shoulder.

The young couple joined Mrs Walker in the living room and chatted over coffee.

'I forgot to tell you both, but I've heard from a couple of

colleges who are happy to accept my enrolment for next year.' he said. Jennifer nodded, and smiled through the uncertainty of what this could mean for her and Jeff's relationship.

'That's great' exclaimed his mum, but added, 'Don't put all your eggs in one basket though.'

'Don't worry mum, I won't.'

Jennifer finished her coffee and then rose to her feet.

'I think it's time I got going.'

'Is your Dad picking you up?' questioned Jeff.

'No, I'll call a cab, can I use your phone?'

'All yours.' he said, gesturing to the cream coloured telephone on the small table. Jen farewelled Jeff's mum, then the couple waited on the porch until the taxi arrived. He kissed her goodnight, smiled, then walked back inside.

| 16 |

Jennifer's accident

As he closed the front door, they heard the screeching of tyres followed by an almighty bang! Jeff raced outside and peered down the road to see two cars involved in a horrific collision. One vehicle was Jen's taxi which was resting on its side!

'Oh my god!' he shrieked and sprinted as fast as he could to the end of the street. It looked as though the other vehicle, a delivery van, had failed to stop at the give-way sign and ploughed into the cab. He heard debris crunching under his shoes as he approached.

'Jennifer!' he screamed. Other residents came rushing out of their houses, some with flashlights. 'Someone call an ambulance!' he yelled.

He peered through the window and turned pale. Both the driver and Jennifer were motionless and splattered in blood. Jeff kicked the windshield in and dragged Jennifer onto the road whilst others attended to the driver. He immediately checked her pulse and she was alive, breathing ever so faintly. Her whole neck and facial area were bloody and bruised. She also had a deep gash along her forehead and her hair was matted with blood. A police car screeched to a halt.

'Hey, this guy's not breathing.' a lady hollered, as she leant over the taxi driver.

A police officer rushed over and attempted to revive him. Two paramedics arrived at the scene and joined in. They worked for some time however the cab driver had suffered a heart attack and could not be revived. Jeff watched two other paramedics work on Jennifer's injuries and then lift her onto a stretcher and into the ambulance.

'I'm coming too, she's my girlfriend.' he said and climbed into the vehicle.

The rescue vehicle sped off with red lights flashing and siren wailing. Jeff looked back to see the driver of the delivery van being put in a police car. The neighbours were huddled in small groups and he noted a jacket had been placed over the deceased taxi driver. His adrenalin was racing as he looked over at Jennifer. She had an oxygen mask affixed to her pretty face. He reached over and held her hand.

Once at the hospital, Jeff provided staff with the details for her admission and then sat dazed in the waiting room. He bought a strong coffee and watched the steam rise from the cup. Thirty minutes or so later, Jen's parents came rushing in and hurried to the admin area.

'Where is our daughter? Can we see her?' shrieked Mrs Moore. Jeff sat there numb with his eyes to the floor. His mum came in to comfort him and he burst into tears. The four of them spent a sleepless night in the waiting room.

At 5:30 in the morning, a doctor by the name of Kadwell updated them on Jen's condition.

'She's in a bad way,' he began. 'She suffered a head injury in the crash and is yet to regain consciousness. It's too soon to say for certain, but she may have also suffered some spinal injuries. She is going to remain in ICU, and we will know more as the day progresses.' he said. They sat there in stunned silence.

'What do you mean spinal injuries?' asked Jennifer's Mum. 'Just what are you saying?'

Dr Kadwell exhaled and then looked at her.

'Well, I'll be straight with you. It may be quite some time before she's walking normally again,' he said. '...and some people who suffer spinal cord injuries may have trouble with balance when they walk, but it is far too early to say at this time.'

Mrs Moore fell sobbing into her husband's arms.

'This is all your fault!' he snapped at Jeff. 'If you hadn't upset her, she never would have gone around to see you.' he blurted. Jeff was stunned.

'It's nobody's fault.' replied Mrs Walker.

'Maybe you'd all better go home and get some rest,' suggested Dr Kadwell. 'We will call you the minute we have an update.'

'No, I'm staying right here.' sobbed Mrs Moore.

'Let's go, Jeff, there's nothing we can do.' said his mum. He rubbed his tired eyes with his hand and looked at the Moore's.

'I didn't cause this.' he said, before walking off with his mother.

He sat in the car and shut his eyes.

'Do you think she'll be OK? She will, won't she? Oh, mum,

what if she cannot walk properly?' he said. 'How can I live with myself?' She held his hand and forced a smile.

'Jeff, it's not your fault. We'll pray she'll be OK, that's all we can do now.' His mother's words of comfort came straight from the heart, having been in a similar situation several years ago. Late one summer's evening, her husband had been killed in a car accident whilst returning home from work. Although most of the scars had healed, Jen's accident had awakened some painful memories.

She spent most of the morning comforting her son, then drove him to the local police station to record his statement.

'The other driver was drunk.' said Jeff when they arrived home. They sat in the garden for the rest of the day until the sun had set. Jeff felt his spirits lift a little.

Before dinner, he telephoned the hospital for an update on Jen's condition. Dr Kadwell informed him that she was still in a coma and that her condition was serious but stable.

'Serious but stable,' he mused, 'that's what they say on TV.'

He went to bed early but not surprisingly, had trouble falling asleep.

'How could this be?' he thought. 'Why now? Why Jen? The only girl I've ever wanted.' He eventually dozed off and after a restless night, got himself ready for school.

'I really don't want to go today.' he said.

'It'll take your mind off things.' replied his mother. She hugged him goodbye and he trudged to the bus stop.

Once on the bus, he was bombarded by questions from Susan and Tracey. He explained to them what had happened but felt drained and was relieved when the bus arrived at school.

Understandably, his mind was elsewhere during most classes and he had trouble focusing. He briefly considered skipping work, yet since he was starting a new role, did not want to let the Cusack's down.

'Hi Jeff,' said Sandy, 'all set to start your new job?'

He nodded. 'I think so.' he replied.

'Let's go and get a coffee.' she suggested. He agreed. 'I read about the accident in the newspaper, how's Jennifer?'

'She's in a coma and severely injured.'

'How are you holding up?' she asked.

'I'm OK. Still in shock, I guess. It was a bad accident.' He paused. 'Her parents think it's my fault. Her Dad saw me leaving your apartment on Sunday morning. That's how this all started.'

Silence.

'I'm sorry Jeff.' said Sandy.

They talked all evening and she explained his new duties to him. Privately, she was concerned about how he was feeling. After work, they went to a quiet café then she drove him home. Before he exited the car, Sandy reached for his arm and spoke.

'If you think it'll help, I'll contact her folks and explain what happened.' He looked at her and smiled.

'Thanks, Sandy, but let's just leave it for now. I hope it won't come to that.'

'How was your day Jeff?' said his mum when he entered the house.

'Average, but it got better as the day progressed. Any news on Jen?' he asked.

'Yes. Mr Moore phoned a couple of hours ago. She is still in a coma, but the prognosis on her spinal injury isn't as bad as they first thought. They think she's going to be able to walk again just fine.'

'That's wonderful news.' he said hugging her.

'You want some more?' she teased.

'What is it?'

'There's a letter for you on your bed.' she replied. He ran to his room and tore open the letter.

'Fantastic!' he cried.

'What is it?' asked his mum.

'It's from The Ashton Times, this is the national competition which Jennifer entered on my behalf.'

'Read it out.' she said.

Dear Jeff,

Congratulations. You have won first prize in the 'Ashton Times Young Poet Competition.'

In addition to the $100 prize money, we take great delight in offering you the chance to join our team as a cadet journalist. This is a wonderful opportunity for both you and our readers, and we hope you will accept our offer of employment.

Initially, you will write a weekly poetry column. You will also be given the opportunity to study journalism at Rinder University, one of the finest in the state. Should you wish to accept our offer of employment, please contact Kimberly Patterson during office hours, within the next fourteen days, on the telephone number listed be-

low. Once again, congratulations. We look forward to working with you!

Robert Tilway, Editor

Jeff was stunned. 'This is amazing!' he shrieked.

'Oh Jeff, a job offer, how wonderful.' said his mum.

'I'm going to Ashton!' he shouted, running around the room, 'and I owe it all to Jennifer' he added, in excitement. 'Let's go and see how she is!' he said.

'Her condition is probably the same, but we'll go anyway.' said his mum.

'I feel so great!' he yelped. 'Dad would be proud.'

His mum nodded and smiled.

They arrived at the hospital, but their smiles quickly faded, when met by Jen's Mum and Dad.

'How is she, any change?' asked Jeff.

'No further news from what I told your Mum this afternoon.' replied Mr Moore.

'Well, it's positive news that she'll walk again.' offered Mrs Walker.

'Is it OK if I see her? asked Jeff.

'I think so,' said Mr Moore. 'Better check with the nurse on duty before you go in.'

Jeff took the elevator to the third floor and located the nurse, who happened to be in conversation with Dr Kadwell.

'Hi, is it OK if I go in for a moment?'

'Only for a few minutes.' replied the doctor. Jeff walked in and was shocked to see his girlfriend in that condition. Jen's head was bandaged, and she was lying on her back with tubes and machines hooked up to her body. He pulled a chair up next to her bed and held her hand. He looked over her pretty face, now cut up and bruised. It was at that moment, the seriousness of her condition hit him. His good news seemed so insignificant. He ran his fingers along her arm as tears welled in his eyes. He held her hand tightly and closed his eyes.

'Please get better Jennifer, I need you.' he whispered. He leant over and softly kissed her on the cheek. 'I love you.' he hushed.

He half-smiled then stood up to leave. He pushed the chair back in place and put on his jacket. Then, something truly miraculous happened. Jennifer's head moved a little and she uttered something which got his attention.

He rushed back over to her bedside.

'Jeff.' she moaned.

'Jen can you hear me?' he said softly, as her eyes began to twitch then slowly open. 'Thank you,' said Jeff looking to the heavens. 'That's another one I owe you.'

He ran to the nurse's station and fetched Dr Kadwell who hurried in to see her.

'Hello there young lady. Just relax and don't try to talk.'

Jeff raced down the stairs and alerted the others, who came rushing into the room excitedly.

'Hi honey,' said Mr Moore. 'We've been so worried about you.' After ten or so emotional minutes the nurse ordered everyone to leave.

'I'm afraid your daughter needs all the rest she can. She's very drowsy anyway. Come back tomorrow when she's more alert.'

Standing in the hospital foyer, Jen's parents were elated.

'We owe you an apology Jeff.' said Mr Moore.

'No, you don't, it's not necessary. It's been a tough couple of days. But everything's going to be OK' he added. Mrs Moore walked over and hugged him tightly.

'Why don't you and your Mum come over to our house for a coffee? she offered.

'That would be nice, we'd love to.' replied Jeff.

The impromptu gathering at the Moore's house was happy and emotional. It also brought them closer together. Tragic events often do that. Jeff told them about his job offer and they were pleased for him.

'Wow, I read the Times every day!' said Mr Moore.

'Yes, I'm so excited, and I owe it all to Jennifer.' said Jeff.

The Walker's exited quite late and were in much better spirits than the previous evening. What a difference 24 hours can make.

'You know,' said Jeff to his mum, 'I think everything's going to work out fine.'

'I told you.' she replied. She smiled and then sighed. 'You've got your heart set on going to Ashton, haven't you? What about me and Jennifer?' Now it was his turn to smile.

'I need to follow this path, and besides Ashton's not that far away.'

'Well, just think everything through. Weigh up all your options.' she added.

But Jeff had already made up his mind. He had been presented with an opportunity and was going to seize it.

'It's not often that you find something you're good at mum, and I enjoy writing. Who knows where it will lead me?'

Once at home, his mind was flooded with words which he shaped into poetry. Inspired by the events from recent days, he wrote a poem titled *Smile = Life,* which he decided to send to the newspaper editor Mr Tilway. He would also present a copy to Jennifer.

Hello out there to all my friends
I hope the sunshine never ends
Remember to walk around with a smile
and if you make someone happy
It makes life worthwhile
So cheer someone up, go and do it today
Make them feel good and show them the way
Life is for living, be happy and share
With friends and family always be there
Feel good about things, feel good inside
Let people in, with an open mind
Take chances in life, you are a long time gone
Learn from mistakes then carry on
Be kind to yourself and to others around
Take time to listen, there's love to be found
Spend time alone with silence or song
Look at achievements, not where you went wrong
Keep an open mind and understand
No one is perfect, not all is planned
All men are equal no matter what race
A smile can be planted on everyone's face

Forgive those few full of hate and greed
Self-happiness in life is all you need
At the end of the day when all's said and done
Be happy and smile, you're number one

Jeff placed the cap on his pen, then typed out his most recent poem.

'That's not bad.' he mused after re-reading the finished product. The moment his head hit the pillow he fell asleep.

| 17 |

Adventure Zone

The next few days passed quickly. Jennifer made steady progress with her recovery and Jeff was settling in well with his new job at the hotel. It was early October when Jen was released from the hospital and Jeff was there to greet her. As they walked to her Dad's car she stopped and hugged him.

'I'll miss you when you go to Ashton.'

A cool, crisp wind blew across his face.

'Hey that's not for a while yet.' he replied. 'We've got to get over our final exams this month before we do anything.' he said cheekily.

'Thanks for reminding me, I've missed so much school-work.' groaned Jennifer.

'Hey, don't worry I'll help you, but you've still got to take it easy.' he replied.

'It's awkward with this neck brace on.' she whined.

'You'll get used to it.' said her father, helping her into the car. When she walked through the front door there was a big 'welcome home' sign hanging in the hallway.

'You like it?' asked Randy proudly.

'Yes, I do.' replied Jen.

'My class made it.' he said, going over to give his big sister a warm hug.

'Not too tight son, Jennifer's got a sore spine.' interrupted his mother.

It took Jen a couple of weeks to get back into a routine, but Jeff, Susan and Tracey were of great help.

The 17th of October was a Monday; it was only seven days until the all-important final exams began. One week of nothing but exams. Although the markings had no bearing on Jeff's position next year, he wanted to finish high school with strong grades, not only for himself but for his parents too.

The mornings were getting cooler and skateboarding to school was dropped in favour of the old rattling bus. He sat next to Tracey, one seat in front of Jen and Susan.

'Only seven days to go,' mused Susan. 'Are you prepared and ready Mr Walker?'

He turned.

'He doesn't have to worry, he's got his career all mapped out, haven't you Jeff?' interrupted Tracey. He grinned.

'Are you gonna do a story on us?' asked Susan.

'How much money you got?' he replied with a smirk. 'I owe it all to Jennifer, she was the one who thought my poems were any good, and she was the one who sent the entry in.' he said, leaning over the seat to kiss her.

'Hey, that's enough of that.' laughed Susan.

'Are we all gonna meet for lunch?' asked Tracey.

'I can't, me and Jen are studying in the library.' replied Susan.

'Me too.' added Jeff.

Tracey scoffed. 'You're all wasting your time. I'd forget it all in a couple of days.' she added. They looked at one another then broke into laughter. 'What's funny?' demanded Tracey.

'Nothing,' said Jen, 'we'll catch you guys later.'

She and Jeff headed to Science class where he greeted his partner Jan.

'You're a star before you know it.' Jan blurted.

'Come again?' he asked.

'One minute, just another struggling high school student, the next, this country's greatest writer!' she finished.

'Alright Jan, what's going on in that unusual mind of yours?' he asked. Laughing, she threw him the current issue of the school newsletter. It featured a story on Jeff's win in the 'Ashton Times Young Poet Competition.' The story was accompanied by a photo and a copy of *Midnight Clouds*.

How did that get in there? he thought, then remembered that Mrs McGill had asked him for a copy.

'It's quite a beautiful poem Walker, I didn't know you had it in you.' said Jan smiling.

'Ha-ha.' said Jeff. Deep down he was proud that his fellow students could learn of his achievement. At the end of Science class, Dave Pender and a cohort walked up to him grinning.

'What's with you Pender?' asked Jeff. The bully sneered.

'What a beautiful poem.' he said sarcastically. 'I used to think poetry was for wimps, but that poem of yours brought a tear to my eye.' Jan watched as her Science partner and Pender glared at each other.

'I'll make that eye of yours black if you don't back off.' said Jeff. He wanted to strike him but didn't. Instead, he did something that often hits harder than a punch. Zipping up his bag, he looked Pender in the face, smiled, then simply walked away.

After Maths and English classes, Jeff met Susan and Jennifer in the library - and Tracey!

'Now *this* is a shock' he said, 'but a pleasant one and it's good to see you here. Hard work pays off.'

'Yeah yeah.' grumbled Tracey. The bell soon sounded, signalling the end of lunch.

'Hey Jeff, wait up,' said Jen, 'I've got something for you.' she added, slipping a folded-up piece of paper into his back pocket.

'What is it?' he asked.

'Just read it when you're alone. I've got to go, see you on the bus this afternoon.'

'I'm working.' he replied, but she had already vanished in the scrum of bodies, all shuffling to their next class. He settled in for his first class after lunch, which was Geography. As the sound of Mr Hibbs voice trailed off in the distance, Jeff unfolded the note from Jennifer and read to himself:

Jeff - just two things:

I love you. Thank you for always being there and for caring about me. I don't think I'll be able to live without you when you go to Ashton, love Jennifer

He broke into a smile.

'Something amusing you Mr Walker?' bellowed Hibbs, from in front of the blackboard.

'No, nothing sir.'

'Is that so?' retorted the teacher as he adjusted his necktie. 'Maybe you'd like to read to the class whatever you've got in your hand.' All eyes quickly focused on Jeff.

'No, I wouldn't sir.'

'Are you aware your exam is taking place in a matter of days? Please don't disrupt other students who would like to do well.' added Hibbs.

Jeff sat quietly and continued to study.

Pleased to see the school day over, he boarded a city-bound bus and bounced into work.

'Hi Sandy, all ready for a busy evening shift?'

'Come with me.' she said in a serious tone.

'What's up?' he asked. She made certain no one was around then whispered to him.

'Alan found out you're leaving and he's not real pleased about it. He was furious. Just letting you know.' she said.

'Maybe I'll go see him.' said Jeff.

'Are you crazy?' replied Sandy.

'Well, the Cusack's have treated me very well. I should do the right thing by them. I'll go and tell him directly that I'm leaving and confirm that the rumour is true.'

He calmly knocked on the office door and seeing that his boss was out, decided to leave a note for him. He was in the progress of searching for a pen when both brothers entered the room.

'Can I help you Walker?' boomed Alan Cusack.

'Ah no, sir, I was just leaving you a note, saying I wanted to speak with you.'

'That's a coincidence because we wanted to have a little chat with you.' replied Alan Cusack.

'Let me handle this Alan,' said Sam. 'Now Jeff, we've heard through the grapevine that you may be leaving us, is this true?' he asked

'Yes, it is.' answered Jeff.

'I knew it!' blurted Alan.

'I've landed myself a journalism job in Ashton, starting early January. Can I add that you've both treated me very well and I've thoroughly enjoyed working at the hotel.'

'Why didn't you tell us?' Sam asked.

'Erm, I've been meaning to, but was a little hesitant.' said Walker.

'Well, the holiday season is fast approaching, and we'd really like you to stay until then.' said Sam.

'Yes, of course I will. I'll finish up in the new year.' he added.

'Good, it's all settled then.' said Sam.

'I'd better get back to work.' said Jeff, walking back to join Sandy in the reception area.

'What happened? Do you still have a job?' she questioned.

'Sure, until the new year anyway.' he replied.

'That's pleasing to hear,' she said. 'I need to visit the post office for a few minutes, can you hold the fort?'

'Sure can.' said Jeff.

He was busy typing when he heard a familiar voice.

'May I get a room please sir?' Jeff swung around to see Rick and Chet grinning from the other side of the counter.

'Hey guys, this is a surprise. How are you?'

'Doing well.' replied Rick. 'We were in the area playing pinball and shopping for records, so thought we'd stop in and say hi. How's Jennifer?'

'Getter stronger each day.' replied Jeff.

'Susan told me what happened to you that night at my place. Sounds wild!' said Rick.

'It was a crazy night and I didn't pull up well the next morning either.' replied Jeff.

They stood and talked for ten minutes when Sandy walked through the front door.

'Hey, who's the fox?' quizzed Chet.

'Sandy, I'd like you to meet some buddies of mine; this is Rick and Chet.' said Jeff.

'Hello.' said Sandy smiling.

'What time do you finish work?' asked Chet, with a smirk.

'Way after your bedtime.' she quipped before sitting down.

'A sense of humour, I like that.' Chet continued, 'Seriously, let me take you to dinner on Saturday night.'

She looked up.

'I am sorry, but I like to date men, not boys.' Jeff stood there hiding a smile. 'Besides, my heart's already taken.' added Sandy, before shooting a quick glance at Jeff.

'He must be something special.' said Chet.

'Yes, he is. Very much so.' she replied, before walking away.

'Are you finished?' asked Jeff, slightly annoyed.

'Wow she's hot!' yelped Chet.

'Ain't it always the way.' said Rick.

'What's that?' asked Jeff.

'I bet the guy who she's flipped for is a real jerk.'

'Yeah,' commented Jeff, 'he probably is. Hey, I've got to get back to work guys. Let's catch up soon.' They shook hands.

'See ya Walker.' said Rick.

'Let me know if that fox wants my number OK?' quipped Chet.

'Sure thing.' replied Jeff with a grin.

He returned to the typewriter and began punching keys.

'Hey Jeff,' said Sandy re-entering the foyer. 'Sam got a letter today from Fournier Management, you know, the Flame crew. They said if they tour the area again, they'll definitely be staying here!' she finished.

'That's cool!' replied Jeff.

'Yes, it's a great endorsement. Sam's already framed the letter and hung it on his wall. But that's not all.' she added, holding up a copy of the band's upcoming album.

'What's that?' asked Jeff excitedly.

'It's an advance copy of the new Flame record, *Scorched City*. Read the liner notes' said Sandy, handing him the album. He scanned the songwriting credits and then got to the 'thankyou' list.

'This is too damn cool!' he said, before reading the words aloud: *'Thanks to Jennifer, Jeff, Sandy and all at the Aaronson Hotel.'* He took the vinyl record out of the jacket and inspected it. 'I cannot wait to hear these new songs. Rock 'n' roll really is a life force isn't it, Sandy?'

She nodded in agreeance.

'Music gives our lives energy. I cannot imagine my life without it.'

The hours ticked by and although the hotel was quiet, there was plenty to do in the office.

'This will take forever!' blurted Jeff, seeing the stack of letters left to type, adjacent the mountain of index cards to be filed.

'There's no rush, just continue when you come in on Thursday,' offered Sandy, 'besides it's time to sign off.' she said tiredly.

'At last, let's get out of here.' he exclaimed.

'Not just yet,' she said. 'There is a gentleman approaching with a girl who I am assuming is his daughter.'

'Terrific,' groaned Jeff sarcastically. 'My long shift is getting even longer.' He looked out the window. 'Hey, they're not guests, that's Jen!' he shrieked, racing outside to greet them. 'What a surprise!' he said, lifting his girl in the air.

'Be mindful of her back Jeff.' said Mr Moore.

'Oops forgot, sorry.' he said.

'Dad and I were on our way home from Gran's, so we thought we'd stop in on the way past.' said Jen.

'It must be the evening for surprise visits, Rick and Chet were here earlier. You're lucky you caught me, Sandy and I were just finishing. Come on in and meet her!' he said.

He walked back into the foyer, but it was empty, deserted.

'That's funny she was here a minute ago.' he said.

'Would you like a lift home son?' asked Mr Moore.

'That'd be super.' He was confused by Sandy's disappearing act but pushed the thought away. 'How's Randy?' he inquired once in the car.

'Always busy. We should have named him 'little Mr Mischief' answered Jen's Dad. 'He talks a lot about you taking him for a ride on that bike of yours.'

'He talks about you a lot.' interrupted Jennifer.

'I'll have to take him fishing or something.' said Jeff.

As the Cordoba moved away from the kerb, Jeff glanced back to see Sandy's red beetle, still sitting in the car park.

'Thanks for the lift Mr Moore.' he said, as they pulled up at his house.

'Goodnight Jeff.' said Jennifer, planting a kiss on his lips. He smiled as he saw her mime three words to him.

'There's a letter here for you from Uncle Jack. It arrived today.' said his mum, putting dinner on the table. She had prepared meatloaf with green peas on the side.

'Smells great.' said Jeff, filling his glass with cola.

'I am glad you are not taking up the school's offer for next year and attending a night college.' she said, placing the oven mitt on the table.

'What's that? Yeah sure.' he replied, whilst reading his Uncle's letter.

'I said I'm glad you've forgotten about that night school idea.' she repeated. Jeff nodded.

'Still at least you would've been close by.' she added, returning to the kitchen for a moment.

'This is great news.' he said, waving the letter.

'What is?' she asked, re-entering the room.

'Uncle Jack said I can stay with him and Brad when I get to Ashton. Just until I get settled and find a place of my own.'

'That's nice of him, why don't you call and say thank you.'

'I sure will.' he replied, delighted with the offer.

He sat talking with his mum for quite a while then went to his room to study.

The next couple of days were fairly typical and uneventful. However, the lunch break on Thursday was livened up by a fight between Dean Mace and Nathan Bennett, two grade eight guys.

'Break it up.' said Principal Green, running across the playground towards the scuffle.

'I'd say Bennett came off second best.' Jeff said to Susan, watching on from nearby. Bennett had blood flowing from a cut mouth, coupled with a swollen cheekbone. Mace on the other hand only had a couple of buttons torn from his shirt.

'What started all this?' demanded Green, marching them both to his office.

'He was bad-mouthing my sister.' blurted Mace. Jeff shook his head and chuckled.

The first thing he did when he arrived at work was to talk with Sandy.

'Hi there.' he said. She smiled. 'You vanished into thin air on Monday night. What happened?' She stared at him.

'I just didn't feel like meeting your girlfriend did I!' she snapped back. He decided not to push the issue and forgot about it. There was not much talk between the two of them for most of the evening. The silence during the shift was bro-ken when he received a telephone call.

'Jeff, phone call for you, another girlfriend no doubt.' said Sandy sarcastically, handing him the receiver.

'Hello, is that Jeff?' asked a female voice.

'Yes, speaking.'

'My name's Kimberly Patterson, I'm from The Ashton

Times. The editor, Mr Tilway would like to conduct an informal interview with you. Next week if possible. He would like to meet you in person and show you around the place.' Jeff was elated.

'Well sure.' he said.

'How about Tuesday at 11:00 AM?' she asked.

'No problem. Oh wait, yes there is, I've got exams all next week.' He could hear Miss Patterson shuffling through papers.

'What about the following Monday? The 1st of November? Eleven again?' she inquired.

'That sounds great. I look forward to seeing you then,' he said. 'Bye-bye.' He jumped out of his chair and hugged Sandy excitedly.

'This is fantastic!' he shrieked, telling her all about his call. She put her head down and frowned.

'Oh Jeff, how will I live without when you're gone?' she uttered. 'My life is so much better with you in it.'

'You'll meet someone special soon. I know you will. You are a beautiful person inside and out.' She put her head to one side and forced a smile.

'We'll write. I promise.' he added.

'Or I can just read the Times.' she replied smiling. They ended the evening with a coffee and then signed off. As soon as he got home, he called the bus company and booked a return ticket to Ashton. Although he was over-excited, he still managed to get some revision done before calling it a day.

He met Jennifer and Tracey on the bus the next morning and told them his news.

'Wow, it's all happening so fast isn't it?' said Tracey.

'Too fast.' commented Jennifer sadly. 'Hey, do you want to come over and study this weekend?' she asked.

'Sure,' said Jeff. 'I was actually thinking of doing something with Randy as well, so I can kill two birds with one stone.' Tracey raised her eyebrows.

'That's a horrible expression.' she said.

'It's an idiom,' said Jeff. 'I like idioms.' Jen playfully tapped him on the shoulder.

'Getting back to the weekend, what did you have in mind?'

'Well let's see, you guys are going shopping on Saturday, aren't you?' They both giggled and nodded their heads at the same time. 'I needn't have asked. I might go to that new amusement park over on the other side of town. It's at Lake Allawah isn't it?' Tracey's eyes widened.

'That's only just opened up. Randy will love it.' she said.

'Not too late though Jeff, we should get some serious study done with the exams so close.' said Jen.

'Don't worry.' he replied, holding her hand. The bus made its way through the suburbs before coming to a stop at the school gates.

If Jeff was seeking homework leniency from the teachers with the exams so close, he was disappointed. He walked away from each of his late-week classes with mountains of the stuff.

'Thank heavens it's Friday. The week really dragged out.' moaned Tracey, on the bus journey home.

'Next week will be worse.' added Jennifer.

'I'm actually looking forward to the exams.' said Jeff confidently. Both girls looked at him with a 'are you crazy?' type stare. 'I'll see you tomorrow.' he said as the bus approached his stop.

'Come here.' said Jen, pulling him by the shirt front. She kissed him gently.

'I loved the note.' he whispered before descending from the bus.

'I have to admit it. He's a nice guy.' commented Tracey.

'I know.' said Jennifer.

'I used to think he was a little weird though.' added Tracey.

'In what way?' asked his girlfriend.

'Well you know, not weird just quirky. He used to always keep to himself, almost as if he were in a world of his own, but that's before we knew him of course.'

'He's creative. His mind was probably working through poems or songs or something. It's who he is.' answered Jen smiling.

'Hey thanks for helping me study this afternoon, I really need help.' said Tracey.

'That's cool, we'll get it all done and then shop until we drop tomorrow.'

Both girls giggled as they got off the bus at Lillivale and were greeted by Randy, playing football in the yard with friends.

'Hi munchkin, did you kick any goals?' asked Jen.

'Nah.' replied Randy.

'Jeff's coming over to see you tomorrow and I think he's got a big surprise planned.'

'Really?! That's neat.' shouted Randy, jumping about with excitement.

Jeff spent the evening playing the advance copy of Flame's

new record, whilst swigging cola and eating candy. He hit the lights and went to bed at 11:00

After coffee and toast for breakfast, he kick-started his Honda and rode over to Jen's house at around 8:00 AM. He was hoping to catch her before she and Tracey headed off.

'Don't tell me I've missed them?' he asked Mrs Moore.

'Yes, they left about twenty minutes ago.'

'Talk about serious shoppers!' he said.

'I was thinking of taking Randy to that new amusement park near Lake Allawah, is that OK with you?'

'Yes, that's fine. He will really love that and it will do him good to have a day out. Just don't let him spend all of your money! Here's ten dollars.' she added, pulling a note from her purse.

'Hi Jeff!' hollered Randy, bounding down the stairs.

'Guess where Jeff is taking you?'

'Where?' he replied enthusiastically.

'To that new amusement park that's just opened up. You're going to Adventure Zone!'

'Cool! Let's go.' he said, darting for the front door.

'Now just a minute young man.' said his mother, pulling him back.

'Please behave yourself for Jeff and don't get into any mischief.'

'Yes Mum.' he replied - the tone of his voice sounding as though he'd heard those words a million times before.

'Don't be home too late!' she yelled, as they made their way to the bus stop.

'We could always ride over there on your bike.' offered Randy. Jeff chuckled.

The day passed too quickly and they both had a lot of fun. Randy was exhausted from all the walking and fell asleep next to Jeff on the bus journey home. Jeff ended up carrying his little buddy off the bus and through the front door of the Moore house.

'Will you look at this?' said Jennifer to her Mother and Father.

'How was Randy?' asked Mr Moore, lifting his head from the newspaper.

'He's had a great day, but now he's wiped out.' replied Jeff, who quietly carried him up the stairs and placed him on his bed.

'He really had an absolute ball.' Jeff added, returning to the living room.

'Thank you so much for taking him out today.' said Mrs Moore.

'No problem.' replied Jeff, pulling two stuffed toys from a paper bag. 'Randy even won this frog at the shooting gallery. But I think the guy felt sorry for him because he missed with every shot.' They all laughed.

'What's the other one?' asked Jennifer curiously.

'This one's for you.' he said, holding up a mustard-yellow coloured bear.

'Isn't he adorable? He is so cute!' she said, clutching it close to her chest. 'His smile is so infectious. I'm going to name him Bobby, he looks like a Bobby doesn't he Mum?'

Her mother looked up from the macramé owl she was creating.

'Oh definitely.' she agreed with a smile.

'Thanks Jeff.' Jen said hugging him.

'Here's your money back Mrs Moore.' he said, placing it on the table.

'Oh, you keep it Jeff, I'd say you earned it today.'

'No really, today was my treat.' he replied, then went to wash up before dinner.

After a filling meal, the two teenagers hit the books and decided to fire questions at one another.

'What's the chemical formula for Nitrous Oxide?' asked Jen.

'Too easy,' he replied, 'N2O. Also known as laughing gas. I need to have some of that stuff handy when I tell a bad joke.' She nodded in agreeance.

'Can I tell you something which is not funny?' she asked. He looked at her.

'I am going to miss you next year Mr Walker.' Jen whispered. She pulled him close to her and they kissed passionately.

'Me too.' he replied, before kissing again. 'But we will be OK, and our love will survive. I'll jump on buses and planes and see you as often as I can' he said. 'I also plan on getting my driver's licence too.' She smiled as her eyes turned watery.

'Better get back to it.' she said, and they continued studying until well after midnight.

Jeff rode home and with a chilly wind biting his face, was glad to get home and wrap himself in his warm bed.

'How was your day yesterday Jeff? I didn't hear you come in last night.' said his mum, at the breakfast table next morning.

'I had a great day with Randy, he's a good kid. Jen and I got a lot of study done last night, but I still have some more to finish today.'

'How do you think you'll perform? Are you confident?'

'Well,' said Jeff, pouring cornflakes into a bowl, 'if I don't know the material now, I never will.' He heard a whistle and despite his bare feet, ran outside to buy the Sunday newspaper from the paperboy. He returned and set it down on the table. 'Ouch' he muttered, rubbing his heels. His mother raised her eyebrows.

'Who knows?' she said, 'I may be reading *your* column this time next year.' pointing to the Times. Jeff smiled and continued with his cereal.

'I'm glad you're home all day because Mrs Preston and I are going to a craft show at the community hall, so I won't have to lock up.' said his mum.

'Did you reply to your Uncle Jack's letter?' she asked, stirring a cup of coffee.

'Sure did. I even enclosed two of my poems.'

'You will try harder to get along with Brad, won't you dear?' He groaned, then continued reading the back of the cereal box.

With the sun streaming down outside, Jeff was tempted to go and read in the backyard. But he instead settled for the corner of his bedroom and immersed himself in his studies.

The shadows soon grew long, and the sun slipped away.

'How was your craft thingy? he asked when his mum arrived home.

'Wonderful. I bought this lovely cream cardigan, what do you think?' she asked, holding the garment up to her chest.

'It's nice.' said Jeff.

After dinner, he took a shower and went to bed early, all ready to tackle the exams.

| 18 |

Mr Tilway

The first exam for the week was English, and Miss Burke's hollering did nothing to put the student's nerves at ease. The all-important end of year exams had begun. The only sounds during the two-hour exam, were the ticking of the clock, the shuffling of papers and the occasional cough.

'Pencils down!' yelled Burke, holding her watch close to her spectacles. Groans and chatter fluttered around the room.

'There will be no talking until all papers are handed in!' the teacher shouted. Jeff felt confident that he'd performed well, except for one or two guessed answers. His next exam was Science which wasn't until after lunch, so he joined a handful of other students, all studying in the library.

'Walker,' uttered librarian Daubney when he entered the room, 'I didn't know you wrote. Congratulations on the poetry competition.'

'Well ahm thanks.' replied Jeff, shaking his hand. Mr Daubney was not particularly keen on Jeff, so this compliment was a little unexpected.

Maybe it's because he digs books, thought Jeff, finding himself a vacant table.

With Pender and two cronies skylarking, the extra revision was a challenge, so he decided to walk to the cafeteria and find Jennifer.

'How did you do?' he asked her.

'Not so great.' she replied. 'It was harder than I expected with some tough questions.'

They walked outside to the grassy area to feel some sunshine.

'We've both got Science this afternoon, so let's cram some revision in now.' said Jeff.

'You can. There is no room left in my brain for anymore revision. It's full.' she blurted.

Jeff spread himself out on the grass and opened his books, but with Jennifer tickling his neck, he found it hard to concentrate. He finally gave in after a few minutes and grabbed her in a playful hug.

'This time next week I'll be on my way to Ashton.' he said excitedly.

Jennifer, trying to hide her disappointment smiled along with him. She didn't want to rain on his parade.

'Where are you staying? In a hotel?' she asked.

'No, with my Uncle Jack.'

'You mean with that jock Brad.' she said, pulling a face.

'I'm afraid so.' said Jeff, as the bell started ringing.

They stood up and brushed the dry grass off their clothes.

'Gee Bulen looks unwell. Really pale.' hushed Jennifer to

Jeff, as they entered the Science lab for their exam. Jeff nodded in agreeance.

'All set?' he said to Jan.

'Absolutely. Future forensic scientist remember?'

He gave her a 'thumbs-up' and smiled.

The papers were handed out and they were away. It was a surprisingly easy exam, or so Jeff thought, and he finished with about ten minutes to spare. The students were busy chatting as they exited the lab and returned to their homerooms. The school day was over.

Two exams down, thought Jeff, as he made his way to the bus lines.

The rest of the week passed quickly, and it was Friday before he knew it.

'They leave the best until last, don't they?' he asked Tracey, referencing the Maths exam later that day.

'Well I'll be glad when three o'clock comes, believe me!' she said.

As is the case with many exams, this one was not particularly difficult - if you had've prepared for it. Jeff tackled the questions positively and although not completing all of them, felt confident he'd performed well. When three o'clock did eventually roll around, the cheer from many students could be heard all over the school. They raced from the building and out of the front gates. Jeff walked slowly and boarded the bus just as it was leaving.

'I'm going over to Susan's tonight to celebrate the end of exams.' said Tracey. Jennifer looked at Jeff.

'Do you want to go to Sue's too? They're having a bit of a party.' Jeff shrugged his shoulders.

'Nah, I'll wait until the big school party tomorrow night.'

'You're not going to that?!' chimed Tracey. 'Only nerds go to those school-organised parties.'

He smiled.

'Guess I'm a nerd then.'

'You should also come tomorrow night.' Jen said to Tracey. 'It won't be so bad.'

Tracey pulled a face and said, 'I'll let you know.'

'So, Jeff, tell us about this meeting in Ashton, is it an interview?' Jen asked.

'No, I think it's more of an informal interview. They just want to meet me and show me around, but I want to make a good impression.'

'When do you go?' she asked

'This Monday, the interview is Tuesday.' he replied.

Happy to get home, he fixed a snack and sat in front of the television just as *Happy Days* was starting.

'How was your Maths exam?' asked his mother entering the house via the front door.

'Fine. I am quietly confident that I did well.' he replied. She carted two brown paper bags, filled with groceries into the kitchen.

'Here's that ribbon you wanted for the typewriter.'

'Thanks, how much do I owe you?'

'It's yours,' she replied. 'Oh, did you call the hotel back?'

'No, why?' he asked.

'There is a message for you by the phone. If it had teeth it would've bitten you!' scoffed his mother.

'I didn't see it.' he said, dialling Sandy's work number. The call was short as things at the hotel were hectic. 'They need me to go in tonight, Max is sick and has gone home.' he said, hanging up the phone.

'I thought you were no longer a hotel porter?' quizzed his mum.

'It's just for one night and hey, I might make a few dollars in tips.'

'Just make sure you have some dinner before you leave.' she said, as Jeff walked away to take a shower.

He felt happy with himself and his life at that moment. Things were looking good. After chomping through three corn cobs and some mashed potato, Jeff called a cab. Jennifer phoned to see if he had changed his mind about going to Sue's.

'I'm sorry Jennifer, but you've just missed him. He's been called in to work tonight.' said Mrs Walker.

Jeff exited the taxi, then hurried into the hotel and changed into his uniform.

'What's up with Max?' he asked Ron, passing him in the foyer.

'He's got food poisoning, I think. He didn't look good.' said the chef.

'I've warned him about pinching food from your kitchen.' said Walker with a smirk.

'Get outta here.' replied Ron, playfully punching him on the shoulder.

'Well someone's in a good mood.' commented Sandy, sauntering past him with a cup of coffee.

'Certainly am.' whispered Jeff, leaning in close to her face. 'I've finished all my exams!' He then backed away and jigged around a little.

'When you've finished that dance of yours, you can carry my luggage from the taxi.' demanded a grumpy old man, standing in the foyer.

'Sorry sir, I'll get them right away.' said Jeff, scooting past him and out the door.

'Room 28.' said Sandy passing the room key to Jeff as he re-entered the hotel.

As Jeff listened to the guest moan about everything from the weather to recent happenings with the government and the military, he wondered just *who* this man was and what was his story.

'I was young once, just like you are now' he continued, 'then before I knew it, my life's gone, just like that. Time is very precious.' finished the man. Although curious, Jeff thought it best not to meddle in a guest's affairs and bid him farewell.

'How is Mr Winthrall settling in?' asked Sandy when he returned.

'He's fine. Is that his name? Winthrall. He's either senile or has an extremely large chip on his shoulder.' commented Jeff.

'Don't tell me you don't know who that is?' questioned Sandy. Jeff shook his head. 'What do they teach you students in history class. That is Sir Richard Winthrall, one of this country's most decorated war heroes.' she said proudly. 'He's in town to give a speech at the museum or something.'

'Really!' said Jeff in awe. He spent his shift recounting some of the things which Sir Richard had said to him. Then he imagined some of the experiences he'd lived through. Yet he was saying that his life had now vanished. Strange indeed.

Just before his shift finished, Jeff decided to check in on Sir Richard and make sure everything was OK.

'What is it?' snapped the guest when he knocked on the door. Jeff was tentative but politely asked if he needed anything.

'Yeah, a decent pillow and another blanket.' came the reply.

'Certainly, sir.' said Jeff exiting the room. He returned five minutes later with the blanket and pillow.

'What's with the 'sir' routine?' asked the guest. Jeff fumbled the pillow. 'My name's not Sir. My Mother and Father named me Richard, not Sir.'

'I'm sorry.' replied Jeff, 'I call most ladies and gentlemen, ma'am and sir.'

'Well you can call me Richard.' he said, with the slight hint of a smile.

Jeff also brought him in a late-night supper, and they chatted for an hour, about life, love, war, and death.

'I'm giving a speech at the museum this Monday afternoon. It'd be nice if you came along son.' offered Sir Richard. Jeff enthusiastically told him about Ashton and the job he had lined up for next year. 'A poet eh? Well, the world needs good poets.' smiled the old man. Jeff returned his smile and exited the room quietly.

Travelling home on the local bus, all he could think about was what an amazing person this gentleman was. He asked his mother about him as soon as he walked in the front door.

'Well sure, I'm familiar with him. Some of your Dad's war books are on the bookshelf. There's bound to be information on Sir Richard in those.'

'Great idea.' he agreed.

As he read carefully about all that this man had achieved, he sat back and smiled, realising just who he had befriended.

'What a great man.' he thought to himself. Inspired, he jotted down a few verses of poetry then went to sleep - a truly fascinating end to a busy week.

The rain poured down for most of Saturday, clearing up late in the day. He phoned Jennifer to arrange details for the school party later that night.

'Did you persuade Susan and Tracey to go?'

'Sue and Rick are meeting us there, and Tracey's still up in the air. She said she may show up later.'

'Great.' he replied.

'My Dad is dropping me off, so we'll pick you up on the way, say 7:00 PM?' offered Jennifer.

'Sounds cool. I'll see you then.' said Jeff.

The evening started off dull with no vibe and no excitement to speak of. The school had hired a disc jockey who kept playing disco and Top 40 songs all evening.

'Play some Rolling Stones!' yelled Jennifer directly in his face. The DJ smiled and nodded.

'I know what we need.' said Tracey who had recently arrived. She casually strolled over to the three bowls of punch and poured copious amounts of vodka from a flask into the fruity liquid. 'That'll get things moving.' she laughed, returning to her friends.

'I'd better go sample some.' said Jeff with a smirk, just as *Jumpin' Jack Flash* by the Stones churned out from the speakers. He turned to find his girlfriend grooving away on the dance floor in rhythm with the tune. He chuckled then gulped down the drink. 'I think I'll have another' he mused as Nick Shinton and a friend approached. 'Have a drink guys, it'll put hairs on your chest!' Jeff said walking away. He laughed aloud when remembering he had none himself!

'How is it?' quizzed Rick. Jeff smiled and winked, then joined Jennifer on the dance floor.

'Finally, the DJ is cranking more rock!' yelled Jen with delight as *Barracuda* by Heart played loudly.

The evening raged on and the party picked up, thanks to Tracey no doubt. Jeff was quite drunk by the time Jen's Dad rolled up at 11:30. He fell asleep in the back of the car and flung himself onto his bed once home.

Fortunately for him, his mother spent most of the next day shopping with Mrs Preston.

He slept until after midday and lay in bed for a while snoozing. The rain falling outside made the prospect of peeling off his blankets even more uninviting.

I'll just lie in a bit longer, he thought, picking a war book up from his bedside table.

'Aren't you up yet!' said his mother, entering the kitchen with her neighbour?

'Yeah, I'm just reading.' replied her son.

'How are you Mrs Preston?' said Jeff, entering the kitchen moments later to make a late lunch.

'You'll spoil your dinner Jeff.' said his mum.

'Congratulations on your job,' said the neighbour, 'Ashton's such a big place.' Jeff smiled.

'Thank you.' he said politely. 'I'll leave you ladies alone.' he added, walking from the room with his sandwich and cola.

He stood peering out from his bedroom window and watched the raindrops slither down the glass. They reminded him of teardrops, sliding down a fragile face. Jeff was soon lost in thought, wondering what the future held for him and remembering what Sir Richard had told him; *the world needs good poets.* After organising his portfolio, he packed his bag and made certain he had everything organised. Sitting at the typewriter he rolled in a clean piece of paper and began a poem. However, after sitting there for over forty-five minutes, he could only manage one verse:

The sky is dark above me, my thoughts are full of you
They soon turn into pleasant dreams
that last the whole night through

He scanned through the pages of an old comic book and then went to sleep.

He awoke early the following day feeling buoyant. His bus to Ashton left the city at 3:00 PM and did not arrive until 6:00 AM the following day. This was due to the bus making stops at small towns on the route. The school exams were over, so attending for a few hours on this particular day seemed a waste of time.

Jeff got to the bus station, checked in and asked for a window seat. He boarded at 2:50 PM and found his seat, adjacent the toilet at the rear of the bus.

'Great.' he mused, as an odour from the washroom's facilities wafted towards him. The Greyhound swung out of the terminal and made its way along High Street, then onto Highway 11. Jeff spent the remaining hours of daylight jotting down poetry. There was a meal break at the small town of Filmark at around 11:30 PM. Walker bought a burger and cola and as the temperature was cool outside, ate his food on the bus.

'This will be our last stop before Ashton.' said the driver over the PA system. He continued talking, but his words became a blur as Jeff reclined his seat back and drifted to sleep. He awoke shivering in the early hours of the morning and slipped on another sweater. He sat with his eyes closed, unable to get back to sleep until they rolled into the outskirts of the big city. It was the first day of a new month.

'Welcome to Ashton ladies and gentlemen.' said the driver, yawning. Jeff sat up and rubbed his eyes.

After fetching his small suitcase, he greeted his Uncle with a handshake.

'Where's Brad?'

'Still asleep.' replied Jack. 'He's not going to get out of bed *this* early. That's asking a bit too much.' he added with a smile.

They walked to the car and travelled for about thirty minutes, passing the Ashton Ale brewery on the way.

'*Wait til I tell the guys I saw that!* said Jeff excitedly, as his Uncle laughed. The Delaney household was a sturdy, two storey home built out of beige brick and situated in the middle-class neighbourhood of Englewood.

The house reminds me of Principal Green's suit, thought Jeff with a smile.

As they trudged along the front path, Jeff studied the dead flower beds, which were overgrown with weeds.

'They need a bit of work.' blurted Jack, pointing to the garden. 'Your Aunt Casey was the gardener in the family.' Jeff felt awkward, unsure of how he should reply.

'Let's get that cousin of mine out of bed!' he said with a smirk.

'Hey Brad, Jeff's here.' hollered Jack, however his son had left to go jogging.

After scrambled eggs and orange juice, Uncle Jack drove his nephew to the city.

'I'll be about an hour or so I reckon.' said Jeff.

Jack drove away and Jeff stood outside the Ashton Times office. It was the tallest building he had ever seen in his life, bigger than anything back home. He arched his head backwards and gazed up at the tower. He walked through the swinging door and scurried into the elevator with a few office workers. He got off on the tenth floor and was greeted by a secretary behind a big desk.

'How can I help you?' she asked. Jeff felt quite nervous and could feel his heartbeat increasing.

'I'm here to see Mr Tilway.'

'Just a moment.' she said and picked up the phone. 'Jeff

Walker is it?' He nodded. 'I'll take you through.' she added, hanging up the phone.

The secretary led him through a winding corridor and into a large office, crammed with paintings on every wall. A tall man in a white shirt and braces walked out of the office.

'You must be Jeff?' he said, 'My name's Robert Tilway, I'm the editor.'

'Pleased to meet you, sir.' said Jeff, firmly shaking his hand.

'Mr Tilway or 'Ed' is fine.' said his new boss. 'Welcome aboard. Come this way and I'll give you a quick tour, show you where you'll be working.' Jeff was shown through two busy floors with people rushing in all directions. Typewriters were tapping and phones were ringing constantly. The sounds were music to his ears and made him grin.

He was also introduced to a couple of sportswriters and the lady who wrote the daily 'help' column, a favourite of his Mum's.

'This will be your desk.' said Mr Tilway, pointing to a small wooden table that was covered in boxes, paper, and a couple of coffee mugs. 'It will, of course, be clean and tidy before you arrive.' added his boss with a smile.

He was then introduced to a military historian called Carol.

'This is the new starter is it Robert?' she asked. 'Lovely to meet you. We have a great team here, poetry is it?' Jeff nodded his head.

'Yes, that's correct.'

'Where are you from?' asked Carol, chewing the end of a biro.

'Key Valley.' replied Jeff. Her face lit up and she smiled.

'Really! I just flew back from that region late yesterday. I went and covered a story on an old general who gave a speech.' she said.

'Sir Richard's an amazing man.' replied Jeff.

'You know of him?! Few teenagers do nowadays.' she said. He nodded. 'Look out for my article later this week.' she added.

'This way Jeff.' motioned Mr Tilway.

'See you around, I hope.' Jeff said to Carol.

'Well what do you think?' asked the boss when back in his office.

'It looks great, I'm very impressed and can't wait to start next year.'

'Ah yes, well I actually wanted to talk to you about that.' began Mr Tilway.

'We've ran the odd story or two about you and your poetry column, and the response has been positive. We would like you to start in four weeks.' Jeff sat back in the chair. 'I know it's a little earlier than we'd planned, but we feel it would be better if you were settled in before Christmas.' he added. Jeff sat there, briefly pondering what the reactions of Jen and his mother would be.

'What would be the proposed new start date?'

'29th of November, it's a Wednesday' replied Mr Tilway. Jeff agreed and they shook hands.

'See my secretary, Miss Patterson, on the way out. She's got some forms for you to complete.'

Jeff thanked him and exited.

Ten minutes later he walked out from the tall structure

and met Uncle Jack who was waiting outside. He told him of his exciting news.

'That's great son. Brad and I are here to help you, remember that.'

'Thanks Jack.' said Jeff as they manoeuvred through the city traffic. His return journey home wasn't until Wednesday and although he could've jumped on a bus later that day, he decided that spending time with his Uncle and cousin was a much more interesting option.

Jeff and Jack were sitting at the kitchen table playing cards when Brad got home.

'Walker!' he blurted, playfully punching his cousin on the shoulder. 'Congratulations on the job. Make sure you whisper in the sports editor's ear, though I'm sure they've already heard of me.' said Brad, broadening his chest.

'No doubt they have.' replied Jeff, raising an eyebrow.

'How's that girlfriend of yours?' asked the stocky footballer.

'She's fine.'

'Tell her I said hello.' said Brad. Jeff smiled and nodded. That was all Jeff saw of his cousin, as Brad then visited a friend's house and returned home late.

Jeff sat in the living room with Jack and proudly showed him some of his work. He enjoyed bonding with his Uncle and valued their time together. It was rare moments like these, where Jeff pined for his Dad. However, having someone like Jack fill a similar role, if only for a moment, made him feel special.

Exhausted, he climbed into a rickety fold-up bed and

drifted off to sleep. During the night, his Dad appeared in a dream and Jeff felt complete contentment.

Uncle Jack roused him from his sleep early in the morning and they made their way to the bus station.

'Say hello to your Mum for me and tell her I'll call on the weekend.' said Uncle Jack, waving his nephew off.

Jeff grabbed a window seat and slid on his sunglasses. There were only a handful of passengers on board and the bus made good time. The driver tuned the bus's radio to a local rock station which made the journey more bearable. Jeff smiled as the on-air DJ played a Wings song. It made him think of Jen.

'Hey rockers don't change that dial, because we've got stacks of black wax, filled with hot tracks a-comin' your way. Time to crank the volume, here are Bad Company.' said the DJ.

Jeff sat up, recognizing the band's name as Sandy had mentioned them. He listened as their song *Movin' On* played over the speaker system. He instantly loved it and tapped his foot in time with the tune. He identified with the lyrics and felt a surge of positivity pass through him as the song played. He took this as a sign that the path he was following was the right one.

It was dark when the Greyhound pulled into the city and Jeff boarded yet another bus to Key Valley. His mother was at the dinner table when he walked in.

'Jeff!' she said, rushing to hug her son. 'You should've called me. I'd have come and picked you up.' He shrugged.

'It's OK, I'm home now.' He put his bag on a chair and opened the refrigerator.

'So how was the trip?' she questioned, eager to find out how the interview went.

'Really good, but I've got some news which is a bit of a shock, maybe you'd better sit down.' The smile on Barbara Walker's face quickly turned into a frown.

'What is it?' she asked.

'Well I'll be starting there earlier than I thought.' said Jeff.

'Just how soon?'

'The 29th of November.' he replied. She stood up and stared blankly into space.

'Aren't you happy for me?' asked Jeff.

'Well of course I am, but it's so soon, and that's your birthday as well.' moaned his mother.

'I couldn't say no to my new boss.' he explained. She was silent for a moment then walked over and hugged him.

'I understand. But it just seems like yesterday I was nursing you to sleep...now you're all grown up.' she hushed. Over a cup of hot chocolate, Jeff told her about his interview and the new workplace. He took a shower and then got ready for the upcoming school day. Before turning in, he walked to the backyard to view the night sky. The air was clear and crisp, a sign that winter was on the way. He gazed at a constellation of stars in amazement.

'Bright and beautiful.' he said aloud, before rubbing his hands for warmth and returning to the house.

| 19 |

Movin' On

Jeff sat with Jennifer on the school bus the next morning and his friends were pleased to see him. It was just over one week until school broke up for the holiday season. There was no point keeping news of his early departure from his girlfriend, although he needed to wait for the right moment. He decided to break the news to her during the lunch break.

They sat next to each other in the cafeteria, waiting for Sue and Tracey to join them.

'Hey Jen,' he began, 'guess what I'll be doing on the 29th of November?'

She flashed him a warm smile and got close to his face.

'Turning seventeen.' she replied.

'Besides that?' he asked.

'Don't worry, I've got a couple of surprises in mind.' she said, playfully pinching his arm.

'I'm starting work at the Times on the 29th.' he said directly. She continued to smile until his sentence had sunk in.

'What! You can't!' she shrieked. 'I thought you were starting in January.' He shrugged.

'Well that's all changed, I found out during my interview.' Jennifer started to sob and hugged her boyfriend.

'Hey, I'll be back in time for Christmas and we'll spend the holiday season together.' he offered, but Jennifer wept softly, and the tears slid down her face.

'I was planning a big party for you.' she sobbed.

'You can still do that.' he reasoned. 'You're happy for me, aren't you?'

Jennifer nodded and forced a tiny smile.

'Come on, let's take a walk.' said Jeff, as they stood and walked out of the cafeteria in each other's arms.

'It's so soon.' she whimpered.

'I know.' replied Jeff, running his hand over her soft face. Jennifer was in a daze for the rest of the day. Jeff was late out of class and then missed the school bus – making Jen feel even sadder. He walked home and collapsed on the sofa. He did, however, find the energy to type a letter to Uncle Jack. After dinner he phoned Jen, hoping to quickly visit, but she was over at Sue's. He sat in bed reading a motorcycle magazine and turned in around ten.

Friday moved at a snail's pace and with only one week to go, Jeff found the routine of school very tedious. Jennifer seemed more settled after having time to digest Jeff's news. Sandy was away, which meant Jeff would be filling her shift that evening. He reluctantly turned down a dinner invitation from Jen, preferring to work, knowing that any extra money would help with his move to Ashton.

It was unusually quiet for a Friday evening - even the restaurant was only half-booked. When his shift was over, he walked from the hotel and was pleasantly surprised to see Jen waiting for him. She was wearing jeans and boots and wrapped in a thick jacket.

'Wanna go somewhere?' she smiled.

'Sure! Now this is a nice surprise.' said Jeff.

'I just don't want to waste our remaining time together.' she said. The couple spent the evening in a café and then huddled together in the park. The fountains were illuminated at night and looked pretty.

'I'm going to miss you when you go.' she said.

'Me too.' replied Jeff. They boarded the last bus for the evening and headed home, agreeing to meet on Sunday. Jen put her head on his shoulder and closed her eyes. A light fog nestled in the suburbs as the bus changed gears and made its way through the quiet streets.

He would indeed miss her.

Jeff and his mum spent most of Saturday giving his bedroom a thorough clean-out.

As he removed the posters from his walls, she inspected a closet drawer.

'I didn't know you had so much junk.' she said, tossing an old football card into the garbage bin. They ate a roast chicken for dinner and afterwards, Mr and Mrs Frawley stopped by for a chat.

Sunday was a glorious day. The morning sunshine weaved through the branches of the trees as their golden leaves sailed away. Jeff loved Autumn, so did Jen, and a picnic at Lake Monohoe was the perfect way to enjoy the day. He rode over to Lillivale and they walked hand in hand to the lake.

'Cleaning out my room yesterday was weird. The reality

that I am leaving is beginning to sink in.' said Jeff. 'Mum was quiet all day too.'

They found a nice flat grassy patch and laid out their blanket.

'Look what I've got!' said Jennifer, pulling a bottle of champagne from the hamper.

'Cool.' said Jeff. 'Courtesy of your Dad's refrigerator in the garage?' Jen nodded and giggled. They nibbled on cheese and fruit, whilst slowly sipping wine. A kestrel flew overhead, skimming the surface of the lake - the sound of its wings like faint breathing.

Jeff produced a book of poetry and Jen listened as he read aloud. The sun was warm and made her feel a little sleepy. She lay on her back with her eyes shut as Jeff ran his hand over her forehead and through her hair. He paused for a moment and whispered in her ear. She smiled. They heard the kestrel call as they embraced. No spoken words were needed. This was a moment in their lives that they would keep near their hearts forever.

The shadows grew long and the wind became colder as it blew through the spinifex grass.

'I guess we should go.' said Jennifer, cuddling him.

'You're right, it will be dark soon.'

As they slowly trekked back to Jennifer's house, there was a pure, heartfelt warmth which radiated between the two of them.

'I love you more than anything in the world.' she said, stopping to hug him.

Monday was the all-important day that the exam results were returned, and most students were understandably apprehensive. For some, a lot was riding on these results, including Jeff, who felt tense when he received the white envelope. This would account for 40% of his grade for the year. He opened it and his eyes quickly caught a glimpse of his Science mark: 75%!

In fact, most of his grades were either above seventy or eighty, except for Maths which was 68%. He was jubilant. He hurried to the bus line eagerly looking for Jennifer. She was standing there with a glum expression on her face. He was quick to hide his smile, sensing her disappointment.

'I failed. Here, have a look.' she said, handing him her results. Most of her scores were around the 60% mark, except for Geography and French, which were over 70%.

'You did great.' he said, but his comforting words fell short of their target.

'I've got to lift my grades next year, I've just got to.' she said.

'You passed and should be proud of your effort.' he said, putting his arm around her. They boarded the bus and discussed their results with Susan, Tracey, and Nick Shinton.

Jeff was elated and bounded through the front door clutching the envelope.

'Close your eyes and hold out your hands!' he said to his mum. She sensed his excitement and did so, then viewed the results. She was thrilled and squeezed him tightly.

'I'm so proud of you Jeff, I really mean it. You are the best son a mother could have.' Jeff felt moved by her comment and returned the compliment.

That final week of school was relaxed and easy. No more homework and plenty of free time. Friday was Jeff's last day of school, and it began the same way as it had for most of his school life - by oversleeping. The weather had turned cold and it was sleeting as he waited at the bus stop. He put his skateboard under his arm and signalled the bus.

It felt strange to walk through those school gates for the very last time. No chance to savour the moment though as the assembly bell had already sounded. Students from all grades had gathered in the hall and applauded as Jeff and his classmates received their recognition certificates.

At approximately 3:00 PM the final bell for the year rang, signalling the end of the school year. A loud cheer echoed throughout the corridors. Jeff took in his last moments of high school by leaning against the lockers and watching the elation unfold. This was a place he'd struggled with early on and he often thought it a waste of time. With no teachers looking, he pulled a black marker from his back pocket and drew the Flame logo on the locker door. He gave a rebellious grin and admired his artwork.

'Sayonara Key Valley High.' he said aloud.

Three kids walked past him, arm in arm, singing the chorus of the Alice Cooper song *School's Out.* Jeff smiled at hearing the lyrics and chuckled. *Indeed, it is,* he thought to himself.

Dave Pender sauntered past and they cast each other a cold stare. Jeff turned, sighed, and slowly walked out of the building. He felt both happy and sad at the same time.

'So that's it for you then.' said Jan, poking him in the ribs.

'I guess so.'

She looked towards the ground, searching for the words to say.

'Take care Walker, you're a nice guy.' He smiled and hugged her.

'I will. You look after yourself too Jan.' he replied. A tear rolled down her cheek and she smiled.

'I'll keep an eye on your newspaper column.' she said, walking away. Jeff felt even sadder.

He placed his skateboard on the road and kicked along home for the very last time. He stopped to stroke a Siamese cat, an animal he'd befriended on his route home from school the past couple of years.

'See ya, buddy.' he said as the cat scurried away when a car approached.

When he entered his family home the smell of roast lamb wafted towards him.

'That smells great.' he said, noticing the shiny cutlery and fine porcelain plates on the table. 'Who's coming for dinner?' he asked. His mum turned and grinned.

'Just you and me.'

It was a magnificent meal, with a rich chocolate pudding for dessert. Jeff and his mother sat talking about his Dad, his childhood, and his future. There were so many cherished memories in that house.

'Jeff,' she began, before producing a shiny object from her pocket. 'Your Father always wanted you to have these but wanted to wait until you were older. I think now is the right time.' she finished.

She dropped her husband's dog tags into their son's outstretched hand.

'Oh, Mum.' he said surprised.

'They were around your Dad's neck every day in Korea, and he was wearing them in the car crash.' she said sobbing. 'He'd be so proud of you now.' They both started crying.

'I miss him so much.' hushed Jeff. There was silence as his mum dabbed at her moist eyes with a tissue.

'Me too.' she sighed. She slipped the tags around his neck and sat back. 'Your Dad is always with you.' she said.

After dinner, Jeff put on a warm jacket and went to the garage to continue his clean-up.

Wrenches, oil pans, grease, spark plugs, fuel, air filters...won't be needing any of that when I'm an Ashton rail commuter, he thought.

He then noted the tent, packed neatly on the shelf and had a great idea. He switched off the light, rushed inside the house and picked up the telephone. He called Jennifer first and then the rest of his friends.

'Let's all go camping next week!' he said excitedly. They all loved the idea.

Early Monday morning, Rick, Susan, Tracey, Jennifer, and Jeff all boarded a bus, bound for Hannowa State Forest. Once at the forest, they stopped in at the ranger's office and bought a map. Although the air was crisp and cool, the sun's rays could still be felt. They hiked for nearly an hour until they all agreed on a campsite.

'Oh, isn't this beautiful?' said Susan, stretching her arms as if reaching for a cloud. 'Smell that fresh air.' she added.

'It's great to be alive.' commented Rick.

After setting up camp, they all went fishing in a nearby stream.

'Did you know that millions of years ago, dinosaurs like the Brachiosaurus inhabited this area?' said Jeff, reading from a guide booklet. He continued sharing information until interrupted by a squeal from Susan.

'I think I've got one!' she shrieked, reeling in her line. Rick quickly grabbed the net and scooped up a good-sized rainbow trout. Sue was quite pleased with her effort and she and Jen were the only ones to land any fish that afternoon. It quickly grew dark and after a short walk collecting wood, Jeff started a fire and began frying their dinner.

'How come you know so much about camping?' asked Rick.

'My Dad taught me.' he replied, then smiled as he felt the dog tags under his shirt. It was a full moon and the five friends sat huddled around the campfire talking and laughing until late.

After four glorious days, none of them wanted to go home, and they reluctantly packed up their gear and returned to the ranger's station. The bond of friendship between the five had strengthened and one thing was certain - Jeff would be missed.

Before they went their separate ways, Jennifer slipped a note inside Jeff's backpack - three verses of poetry which she had copied from a book. He found it on Saturday whilst doing some laundry. He curiously unfolded the paper and read it:

Jeff, it's time I gave <u>you</u> some poetry:

Please don't forget me when you are gone
Your light in my heart is always on
I'm asking you, darling, with all of my heart
Remember I love you when we're apart
I need you more than ever and want you to know
We'll always be together
Never let each other go

                   love Jennifer

He smiled at Jen's heartfelt message and the words she'd chosen. He read it a second time then placed the note in an old shoe box, along with some other treasured items.

Jen phoned later that afternoon and persuaded him to join her at her house. Since this was their last chance to say good-bye, his friends had planned a little get-together of their own. It was a pleasant evening and more tears were shed.

'You are my best friends.' said Jeff. 'We've created some wonderful memories together and I'm proud to know you.' He also said goodbye to Mr and Mrs Moore, thanking them for all they had done for him.

'Randy will be upset he missed you.' said Mrs Moore. 'He's at his grandmother's all weekend.' Jeff smiled.

'I'll see him at Christmas and maybe even take him for that ride.' offered Jeff.

He went to work at the hotel on Monday and Tuesday. Sandy looked more beautiful than ever and he was pleased to see her. After his Tuesday night shift, the hotel staff all gathered in the bar and gave him a small farewell party. Sam Cusack gave a speech and presented him with a silver pen. It had his name engraved on it. Jeff was not expecting anything like this and had a hunch that Sandy had a hand in it. He sat next to her and whispered in her ear.

'Thank you, you're a beautiful person.' She smiled and held his hand.

'I'm going to miss you, Jeff.' she hushed. 'My feelings for you are still the same.'

Jeff returned her smile.

'I really wish things could've been different. Maybe our paths will cross again in the future.' he said, holding up his glass. 'To us and to happiness.'

She smiled as their glasses clinked.

'I will always carry you in my heart.' she whispered.

She drove Jeff home in her beetle.

'You know, whenever I see a red Volkswagen, I'll always think of you.' he said smiling. They hugged for a long time.

'I'll never forget you.' she said, before he got out of the car.

'Take care.' he replied. He turned then walked away, resisting the temptation to look back at her. Her engine was still running as he opened the front door.

'How was work today?' asked his mum.

'Great. They had a farewell party for me and gave me a nice gift too.' He moved the curtain in time to see Sandy's beetle, gently pull away.

'I was worried when you took that job, but it all worked out OK in the end.' said his mum.

'I've got a lot of nice memories.' said Jeff, watching the glow of Sandy's tail lights disappear in the darkness. After a shower, he sat in front of the TV drinking cola and eating chocolate. He caught the end of the midnight movie then went to bed. Although tired, he had trouble falling asleep. He thought over his relationship with Sandy and what could have been. In another time and place, who knows? Jeff hoped he would see her again.

He was packing some clothes early Wednesday when there was a knock at the door.

'Hey buddy, just wanted to stop by before you go.' It was Bill. 'Here I've got something for you.' he said, giving him a card. It was from the Frawley family wishing Jeff the best of luck.

'Please thank them for me.' he said. They sat and laughed all afternoon, whilst Jeff continued his packing. 'Remember this?' he said, throwing Bill a cane.

'Now that brings back some memories. The Principal's cane. I never thought you had the nerve to steal it.' said Bill, feeling it with his hands.

'Well with the number of times I copped it, especially early on - I felt it was rightfully mine.' laughed Jeff.

'Keep in touch huh?' said Bill rising to his feet.

'I will.' replied Jeff.

'When do you depart?' asked his friend.

'This Friday. I'll be back for Christmas.' They shook hands and Jeff watched him ride away on his bicycle. He smiled. They had grown up together and even though they were not always close, Bill was always there.

On Thursday afternoon, Mrs Walker watched her son load his possessions onto an Ashton bound removal truck.

She stood at the living room window with her hands in her pockets. He saw her sullen face and walked back inside.

'Mum, I'm not going to Mars, please don't get upset.'

'I'm sorry Jeff, I can't help it.'

By the time he went to sleep, everything was done, and he was ready to go. He tossed and turned that evening and found it difficult to sleep. He fetched a drink from the kitchen and knocked on his mother's bedroom door before entering.

'Mum.' he whispered.

'I'm awake Jeff. I can't sleep either.' She told him how much she loved him and re-assured herself that everything was going to be OK, but that she did not want to live alone. Jeff hugged her then kissed her goodnight.

'I'll always be there for you.' he whispered. He went back to bed and eventually fell asleep.

After cereal and toast for breakfast, it was time for him to leave. He picked up his bags and stood for a moment, staring at his bedroom. He could feel a lump in his throat but pushed it away with a deep breath.

'Let's go.' he said, hastily walking from the house to the car.

The telephone was ringing.

'I'll answer it.' he said, running back inside. It was Jennifer, saying one last goodbye.

'I love you, Jeff.'

'I love you too angel.' he whispered, as a tear rolled down his face. He hung up, smiled at the photograph of his Dad adjacent the phone, then left.

It began to rain, and Jeff sat in silence as his mum drove

him to the bus terminal. They were both crying when he boarded his Ashton-bound bus. She watched him wave from the window as the coach pulled away. He felt a little nauseous and shut his eyes, resting his head against the glass.

His mother drove home in a daze then parked her car in the garage. She glanced at her husband's old army tent that sat folded on a shelf. In front of the shelf stood Jeff's red motor-cycle.

She shook the water from her umbrella and left it on the porch. The house felt cold when she opened the front door. She paused for a moment and then sighed. She walked along the hallway and then stood weeping in her son's room. The emptiness of the walls, matching what she felt inside.

Jeff was gone.

Flame concert poster

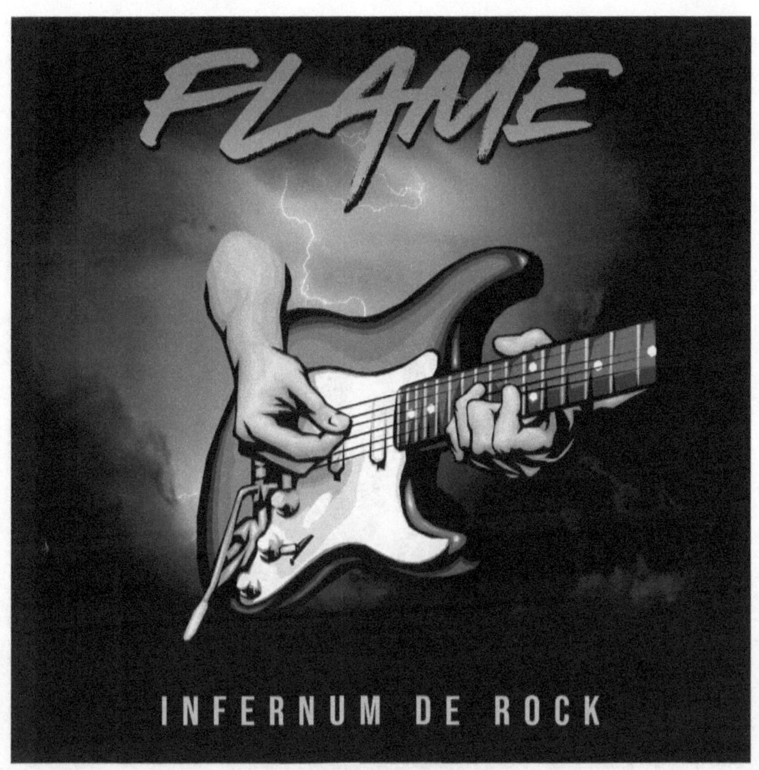

Flame's album 'Infernum De Rock'

Ashton Ale - 'the beer that made Ashton famous'

Denis Gray was born and raised in Sydney, Australia. He has spent most of his life listening to music and reading books, and is particularly fond of rock 'n' roll biographies and inspirational poetry. He enjoys many musical genres and is equally at home if attending a loud rock concert - or listening to his Melanie records. Denis also digs motorcycles and podcasting.

www.denisgray.com

www.ingramcontent.com/pod-product-compliance
Lightning Source LLC
Chambersburg PA
CBHW050203120726
47903CB00002B/737